The time had come. He was about to be measured.

He looked around and saw that it was impossible to escape from his regiment, which enclosed him. Tradition and law also boxed him in. He told himself that he never had wanted to come to the war; he hadn't willingly enlisted; the merciless government had dragged him into this, and now they were taking him to be slaughtered.

A Background Note about
The Red Badge of Courage

The Red Badge of Courage takes place during the US Civil War (1861–1865) between the Union (North) and Confederacy (South). The North sought to preserve the union of all states and end black enslavement. The South wanted to separate from the rest of the United States and keep slavery. Union soldiers, who wore dark blue, called Confederate soldiers "Johnnies" and "rebels." Confederate soldiers, who wore gray, called Union soldiers "Yanks." To this day more US citizens died in the Civil War than in all other wars combined: over 600,000.

The novel describes experiences of the Union's Army of the Potomac. In historical terms the book's winter camp is the Union camp at Falmouth, Virginia; Henry Fleming's regiment is the 124th from Orange County, New York; and the conflict is the Battle of Chancellorsville, fought in northern Virginia in May 1863. The Union troops lost the battle, in which an estimated 24,000 men died.

★★★ THE ★★★
RED BADGE OF COURAGE

STEPHEN CRANE

Edited, and with an Afterword,
by Joan Dunayer

 THE TOWNSEND LIBRARY

THE RED BADGE OF COURAGE

TP **THE TOWNSEND LIBRARY**

For more titles in the Townsend Library,
visit our website: **www.townsendpress.com**

All new material in this edition is
copyright © 2005 by Townsend Press.
Printed in the United States of America

0 9 8 7 6 5 4 3

Illustrations © 2005 by Hal Taylor

Townsend Press, Inc.
439 Kelley Drive
West Berlin, New Jersey 08091
cs@townsendpress.com

ISBN-13: 978-59194-050-0
ISBN-10: 1-59194-050-8

Library of Congress Control Number:
2005924143

CONTENTS

CHAPTER
1

The cold passed reluctantly from the earth. The retiring fog revealed the Union's Army of the Potomac stretched out, resting, on the hills of Falmouth, Virginia. As the landscape changed from brown to green, the army awakened and began to tremble with eagerness at the distant sound of gunfire. The army looked at the roads, which were growing from long troughs of liquid mud to proper thoroughfares. Amber-tinted in the shadow of its banks, the Rappahannock River flowed at the army's feet. At night, when it had become sorrowfully black, the red gleam of Confederate campfires showed in distant hills south of the river.

Jim Conklin, a tall Union soldier, went to wash a shirt in a brook. He came flying back, waving his garment like a banner. He was bursting with a tale he had heard from a reliable friend, who had heard it from a cavalryman, who had heard it from his brother, an orderly at division headquarters. Jim adopted a herald's important air. "We're going to move tomorrow," he said pompously to a group in his camp. "We're going to go way up the river, cut across, and come around behind them."

Jim loudly told his attentive audience about a brilliant, elaborate plan. When he finished, the blue-uniformed men scattered into small arguing groups between the camp's rows of squat brown huts. A black wagon-driver who had been dancing on a cracker box was deserted by the dozens of soldiers who had found him hilariously entertaining. He sat down mournfully. Smoke drifted lazily from many quaint chimneys.

"It's a lie," private Ned Wilson said loudly. His smooth young face was flushed. His hands were thrust sulkily into his pants pockets. He was offended. "I don't believe this damn army is ever going to move. I've gotten ready to move eight times in the last two weeks, and we haven't moved yet."

Jim felt called on to defend the truth of the rumor that he had introduced. He and Ned came close to fighting over it.

A corporal began to swear. He had just added a costly floor to his house, he said. With the arrival of spring he had refrained from making his house more comfortable because he had felt that the army might go on the march at any moment. Lately, however, he'd gotten the impression that he was in a sort of eternal camp.

Many of the men engaged in a spirited debate. One outlined all the plans of General Joseph Hooker, the commanding general. Other men insisted there were other plans. The two sides clamored at each other. Meanwhile, Jim bustled about importantly, assailed by questions.

"What's up, Jim?"

"The army's going to move."

"What are you talking about? How do you know it is?"

"You can believe me or not. I don't give a damn."

Henry Fleming, a young private, eagerly listened to Jim and the others. After receiving his fill of discussions on marches and attacks, he went to his hut and crawled through the hole that served as a door. He lay down on a wide bunk that stretched across one end of the room. In the other end, cracker boxes served as furniture. They were grouped around the fireplace. On the walls were a picture from a weekly newspaper and three rifles arranged in parallel on pegs. Other equipment hung on projections. Some tin dishes lay on a small pile of firewood. A folded tent served as a roof. The sunlight above it made it glow light yellow. A small window allowed a square of whiter light to fall on the cluttered floor. At times smoke from the fire wreathed into the room instead of going out the flimsy chimney of clay and sticks.

Henry was in a sort of trance. At last they were going to fight. Tomorrow, maybe, there would be a battle, and he would be in it. He had dreamed of battles all his life—vague conflicts of thrilling sweep and fire. He had imagined himself bravely protecting people and gaining glory. Several times he had burned to enlist. He had read of marches and battles and had longed to see it all. But his mother had discouraged him. With deep conviction she had dismissed his war ardor and patriotism. Sitting calmly, she had given him many reasons why he was vastly more important on the farm than on the battlefield. Finally, however, the newspaper reports of decisive victories, the village gossip, and his own imagination had aroused Henry too much to resist.

One night as he lay in bed, Henry had heard the church bell ringing to announce news of a great battle. He had shivered with excitement. He had gone down to his mother's room and said, "Ma, I'm going to enlist."

"Henry, don't be a fool," his mother had replied. She then had ended the discussion by covering her face with her quilt.

Nevertheless, the next morning Henry had gone to the nearby town of Port Jervis, New

York and enlisted. When he had returned home, his mother had been milking a cow while four other cows stood waiting. "Ma, I've enlisted," he had said shyly.

After a short silence, his mother had replied, "God's will be done, Henry." Then she had continued to milk the cow.

When Henry had stood in the doorway in his uniform, his eyes lit with excitement, he had seen two tears leave trails on his mother's cheeks. She had disappointed him by saying nothing about his returning a hero. Instead she had continued to peel potatoes and had said, "You watch out, Henry, and take good care of yourself. Don't think you can lick the whole Confederate army. You're just one little fellow among many others. Keep quiet, and do what they tell you. I've knit you eight pairs of socks and put in all of your best shirts. I want you to be as warm and comfortable as anyone in the army. Be careful about the company you keep. There are lots of bad men in the army. The army makes them wild, and they like nothing better than to teach a young fellow like you to drink and swear. Stay clear of those men. Don't ever do anything that you would be ashamed for me to know about. Think of me as watching you. Always remember your father, too. Remember that he never drank a drop of liquor and seldom cursed. I don't know what else to tell you, Henry, except that you mustn't ever do something wrong for my sake. If a time comes when you have to either do something wrong or be killed, do what's right. Many women have to bear up after the loss of their husbands and sons. God will take care of me. Now, don't forget about the socks and shirts. And I've put a cup of blackberry jam with your bundle because I know you like that more than anything else. Goodbye, Henry. Watch out, and be a good boy."

Henry had been impatient during her speech, which had irritated him. He had left feeling relieved not to hear more. But when he had looked back from the gate, he had seen his mother kneeling among the potato parings. Her brown face, upraised, had been stained with tears, and her spare form had trembled. He had bowed his head and gone on, suddenly feeling ashamed.

Henry had gone to his school to say goodbye to his schoolmates. They had crowded around him with wonder and admiration. He had swelled with pride and strutted in his uniform.

One light-haired girl had made fun of his military spirit, but a darker girl whom he had gazed at had seemed to grow shy and sad at the sight of his uniform. As he had walked down the path between rows of oaks, he had turned his head and detected her at a window watching his departure. She immediately had averted her glance. Since then he had thought of her often.

On the way south to Washington, DC, Henry's spirits had soared. His regiment, the 124th New York, had been fed and caressed at station after station until he had believed himself a hero. There had been a lavish expenditure of bread, cold cuts, coffee, pickles, and cheese. Basking in young women's smiles and old men's compliments, he had felt capable of mighty deeds.

After complicated travels with many pauses, there had come winter months of monotonous camp life in Falmouth, Virginia. Henry had believed that war was a series of death struggles with little time in between for sleep and meals. However, since his regiment had come to the field, the army had done little but sit and try to keep warm.

Henry had come to see himself as simply part of a vast uniformed demonstration. He was drilled and drilled. His job was to try to be comfortable.

The only Confederates he had seen were some guards along the Rappahannock's southern bank who sometimes shot at the Union guards on the river's northern side. When reproached for their shots, they usually apologized and swore that their guns had gone off unintended. One night when he was on guard duty, Henry had conversed with one of the Confederate guards, a slightly ragged man who would spit between his shoes and whom Henry had liked.

"Yank," the Confederate soldier had called to him, "you're a damn good fellow."

That statement of approval had made Henry temporarily regret the war.

Various veterans had told Henry tales. Some spoke of whiskered gray hordes who bravely advanced, chewing tobacco and cursing. Others spoke of tattered, hungry men who fired without conviction. Veterans talked much of smoke, fire, and blood, but Henry couldn't tell how much was lies. Because he was a new recruit, they often yelled "Fresh fish!" at him.

Henry now lay in his bunk trying to convince himself that he wouldn't run from a battle. Fear grew in his mind. As he imagined himself actually moving forward to fight, he saw hideous possibilities. Would he stand stoutly? He recalled his visions of broken-bladed glory, but those visions dissolved in the shadow of the coming battle. He sprang from his bunk and paced. "Good Lord, what's wrong with me?" he said aloud.

After a time Jim slid through the hole. Ned followed. They were arguing.

"That's all right," Jim said as he entered, waving his hand dismissively. "You can believe me or not."

Ned grunted stubbornly. For a moment he seemed to be searching for an unassailable reply. Finally he said, "Well, you don't know everything in the world."

"I didn't say I know everything in the world." Jim began to put various articles snugly into his knapsack.

Pausing in his nervous walk, Henry looked at Jim. "There's going to be a battle, Jim?"

"Yes. Just wait until tomorrow, and you'll see one of the biggest battles ever."

"Huh!" Ned scoffed from a corner.

"Well," Henry said, "this rumor probably will turn out like the others did."

"No, it won't," Jim said, exasperated. "The cavalry started this morning. They're going to Richmond while we fight the Johnnies."

Henry remained silent for a time. At last he said, "Jim."

"What?"

"How do you think our regiment will do?"

"We'll fight all right, I guess, after we get into it."

"Do you think any of the boys will run?" Henry asked.

"A few maybe, but there's that kind in every

regiment, especially when they first go under fire. Of course, the whole regiment might turn and run if some big fighting comes right at the beginning. Then again, we might stay and fight like all hell. You can't bet on anything. We haven't been under fire before. Probably we'll fight better than some and worse than others."

"Did you ever think you might run, Jim?" Henry asked. Then he laughed as if he had intended his question to be a joke. Ned also giggled.

Jim waved his hand. "Well, I've thought it might get too hot for me in some of those battles and that if lots of boys started to run, I'd probably run too. If I did start to run, I'd run like the devil. Make no mistake. But if everybody stood and fought, I would too."

Henry was grateful for Jim's words. He had feared that all of the untried men possessed great confidence. He now was somewhat reassured.

CHAPTER
2

The next morning Henry discovered that Jim had been the fast-flying messenger of a false rumor. Many of the men mocked Jim, who fought with one man and beat him severely.

Henry remained agitated by fears that he might run away in battle. He continually tried to measure himself against others. Jim gave him some assurance. He had known Jim since childhood. If Jim could be confident and largely unconcerned, surely he could too. Still, Henry would have liked to know that some other soldier felt self-doubt. Whenever he hinted at the subject, he failed to bring forth any confessions. At times he imagined all of the other soldiers to be brave. At other times he assured himself that they all were privately fearful. When other men spoke eagerly of a prospective battle, he often suspected they were lying.

Henry became anxious to settle the question of his own bravery. He found the generals' slowness intolerable. They seemed content to sit tranquilly on the river bank. Sometimes he felt so angry toward the generals that he grumbled around the camp like a veteran.

One April morning before daybreak, Henry heard trampling off in the darkness. His regiment stood at rest for what seemed a long time. Henry began to believe that at any moment the ominous distance would blaze and crash with combat. He looked at Colonel MacChesnay on his horse. MacChesnay lifted his large arm and calmly stroked his mustache.

At last Henry heard a horse's galloping hoofs. It must be the coming of orders. He bent forward, scarcely breathing. The clickety clack of the horse's hoofs grew louder and seemed to beat on Henry's soul. A horseman with jangling equipment drew up in front of MacChesnay. The two held a short, sharp-worded conversation. The men in the foremost ranks craned their necks.

As the horseman wheeled his horse around and galloped away, he turned to shout over his shoulder, "Don't forget that box of cigars!"

MacChesnay mumbled in reply.

Henry wondered what a box of cigars had to do with war.

A moment later the 124th went swinging off into the darkness. It was now like a moving monster with many feet. The air was heavy and cold with dew. The regiment marched across wet grass. Creakings and grumblings came from the road as some guns were dragged away.

The men stumbled along, muttering speculations. There was a subdued debate. Once, a man named Bill Smithers fell down. As he reached for his rifle, a comrade accidentally stepped on his hand. Bill swore bitterly. A number of the men tittered.

The men passed into a roadway and marched forward with easy strides. A dark regiment moved before them. The tinkle of equipment on the bodies of marching men came from behind, too.

The sky was increasingly yellow. When the sun's rays brightened the earth, Henry saw that the landscape was streaked with two long, thin black columns. One end of the columns disappeared over the brow of a hill; the other vanished in a wood.

Henry felt sullen and despondent. He looked ahead, expecting to hear the rattle of firing. But the black columns crawled from hill to hill without bluster or smoke. A dust cloud floated away to the right. The sky overhead was blue.

Henry studied his companions' faces, hoping to detect emotions like his own. He was disappointed. The men looked almost gleeful.

They spoke of certain victory. Henry felt separate from the others. The regiment tramped to the tune of laughter.

A fat soldier attempted to steal a horse from a house's dooryard. He planned to load his knapsack onto the horse. He was escaping with his prize when a girl rushed from the house and grabbed the horse's mane. A struggle followed. Standing at rest in the roadway, the entire regiment became engrossed in the struggle and seemed to forget their own, much larger battle. They jeered at the fat soldier, hurled insults at him, and enthusiastically supported the young girl. One soldier called to her, "Hit him with a stick!" When the soldier retreated without the horse, the regiment rejoiced, showering catcalls on him and congratulations on the girl, who stood panting and regarding the troops with defiance.

At nightfall the column broke into regiments, which went into the fields to camp. Tents sprang up like strange plants. Campfires dotted the night like peculiar red blossoms.

Henry avoided conversation. He wandered some distance away and looked back at the campfires. The black forms of men passing to and fro before the crimson rays looked weird and satanic.

Henry lay down in the grass. The blades

pressed tenderly against his cheek. The moon hung in a treetop. The night's stillness enveloped him. He vastly pitied himself. The caressing breeze seemed an expression of sympathy. He wished that he were home making the endless rounds from house to barn, barn to fields, fields to barn, and barn to house. He remembered that he often had cursed the cows and sometimes had flung the milking stool. From his present perspective, there was a halo around each of their heads. He would have sacrificed all the brass buttons on all the uniforms in the world to return to them. He told himself that he wasn't cut out to be a soldier, that he radically differed from the other men.

Hearing the grass rustle, Henry turned his head and saw Ned. He called out, "Wilson!"

Ned approached. "Henry? What are you doing here?"

"Thinking."

Ned sat down and lit his pipe. "You look downcast. What's wrong with you?"

"Nothing."

Ned launched into the subject of the anticipated fight. "We've got them now!" His boyish face was gleeful. His voice had an exultant ring. "We'll lick them good!" Then he added more soberly, "Actually, they've licked *us* in just about every battle up to now. But this time we'll lick them good!"

"A little while ago you objected to this march," Henry said coldly.

"I wasn't complaining about marching," Ned said. "I don't mind marching if there's fighting at the end of it. What I hate is getting moved here and there with nothing coming out of it except sore feet and reduced food rations."

"Well, Jim says we'll get plenty of fighting this time."

"He's right for once. We're in for a big battle, and we've got the best end of it. We'll thump them!" He rose and began to pace excitedly. His enthusiasm gave him an elastic step. He was sprightly, vigorous, and fiery in his belief in success.

Henry watched him for a moment in silence. Then he said bitterly, "You're going to do great things, I suppose."

Ned blew a cloud of smoke from his pipe. "I don't know," he said with dignity. "I suppose I'll do as well as the rest. I'm going to try like thunder." He seemed proud of this statement's modesty.

"How do you know you won't run when the time comes?" Henry asked.

"Run? Of course I won't run!" Ned laughed.

"Plenty of men have thought that they'd do

great things before a fight, but when the time
came they ran."

"I guess that's true, but I'm not going to
run. The man who bets on my running will lose
his money." Ned nodded confidently.

"Who do you think you are, the bravest
man in the world?"

"No," Ned said indignantly. "I didn't say
that I'm the bravest man in the world. I said
that I'm going to do my share of fighting. And
I will, too. Who are you, anyhow? You talk
mighty big for someone who hasn't even been
in battle." He glared at Henry and then strode
away.

Henry called after him, "You needn't get
mad about it."

Ned continued on his way and didn't reply.

Henry felt more alone than before. His fail-
ure to discover any resemblance between his
feelings and Ned's made him more miserable.
He went slowly to his tent and stretched himself
on a blanket alongside Jim, who was snoring.
He stared at a campfire's red, shivering reflec-
tion on his tent's white wall until, exhausted by
his own fretting, he fell asleep.

CHAPTER
3

The next night, the regiments filed across two bridges. Henry felt they might be assaulted from the woods at any moment. He eyed the darkness. But his regiment went unmolested to a camping place, where the soldiers slept the sleep of weary men.

In the morning the men were roused early and hustled along a narrow road that led deep into the forest. During this rapid march the 124th lost many of the marks of a new regiment. The men had begun to count the miles. They grew tired. "Sore feet and damn short rations," Ned complained. The men perspired and grumbled. They began to shed their knapsacks. Some tossed them down indifferently; others hid them carefully, hoping to return for them at some future time. Men took off thick shirts. Presently few carried anything other than their necessary clothing, blankets, haversacks, canteens, arms, and ammunition.

The 124th wasn't veteran-like in appearance yet. Veteran regiments usually were small groups. Once, when the 124th had first come to the field, some passing veterans had asked them, "What brigade is this?" When the men had replied that they were a regiment, not a brigade, the older soldiers had laughed and said, "My God!" Also, the hats of the 124th all were the same style instead of showing changes in head-gear over a period of years, and none had letters of faded gold.

One gray dawn Ned kicked Henry in the leg. Before he was fully awake, Henry found himself running down a road amid men who were panting from speed's first effects. His canteen banged rhythmically on his thigh. His haversack bobbed softly. At each stride his musket bounced slightly from his shoulder and made his cap feel uncertain on his head.

Henry could hear the men whisper jerky sentences. "Say . . . what's all this . . . about?" "Why the thunder . . . are we . . . hurrying?" "Billie . . . keep off my feet. You run . . . like a cow."

A sudden spatter of firing came from the distance. Henry was bewildered. As he ran with his comrades, he tried to think, but all he knew was that if he fell down, those coming behind would tread on him. The sun spread revealing rays. One by one, regiments burst into view. Henry knew that the time had come. He was about to be measured. He looked around and saw that it was impossible to escape from his regiment, which enclosed him. Tradition and law also boxed him in. He told himself that he never had wanted to come to the war; he hadn't willingly enlisted; the merciless government had dragged him into this, and now they were taking him to be slaughtered.

The 124th slid down a bank and wallowed across a small stream. As they climbed the hill on the farther side, artillery began to boom. Henry suddenly felt curious. He scrambled up the bank, expecting a battle scene. There were some small fields surrounded by forest. Waving lines of skirmishers spread over the grass and in among the trees. The skirmishers ran here and there, firing into thickets and at distant trees. A dark battle line lay upon a sun-struck clearing. A flag fluttered.

Other regiments floundered up the bank. The brigade was formed into a battle line. After a pause they started slowly through the woods in the rear of the receding skirmishers.

Henry tried to observe everything. He wasn't careful to avoid trees and branches. His forgotten feet repeatedly knocked against stones and got tangled in briers.

Once, the line encountered the body of a dead soldier. He lay on his back staring at the sky. He was dressed in an awkward suit of yellowish brown. The soles of his shoes had been worn to the thinness of writing paper. A foot projected from a large rip in one of the soles. Fate seemed to have betrayed the soldier, exposing his poverty to enemies and friends alike. The ranks opened to avoid the corpse. Henry looked at the ashen face. The wind lifted the reddish-brown beard, which moved as if a hand were stroking it. Henry felt a desire to circle the body and stare at it, to find some answer in the dead man's eyes.

Suddenly Henry felt threatened by the peaceful landscape. A coldness swept over him. A house standing peacefully in distant fields looked ominous. He felt that fierce-eyed enemies lurked in the woods. He suddenly thought that the generals didn't know what they were doing. It all was a trap. The close forests would erupt with rifle barrels. Iron-like brigades would appear in the rear. They all were going to be sacrificed. The generals were stupid. The Confederates would swallow the entire brigade. Henry thought he must break from the ranks and warn his comrades. They mustn't be slaughtered like pigs. But his outcry stayed in his throat. Even if the men were tottering with fear, they would laugh at his warning. They would jeer him, possibly even pelt him.

The line went calmly on through fields and woods. Henry looked at the men nearest to him. They looked deeply interested, as if they were investigating something fascinating. One or two stepped in an overly bold way, as if they already were plunged into war. Others walked as on thin ice. Most of the untested men looked absorbed.

Henry lagged, with tragic glances at the sky. Charles Hasbrouck, the company's young lieutenant, began to beat him with a sword, shouting, "Come, young man. Get up into the ranks. No skulking." Hating Hasbrouck, Henry hastily mended his pace.

After a time the brigade was halted in the cathedral light of a forest. The skirmishers still were firing. Smoke from their rifles floated through the aisles of the woods.

During this halt many men in the 124th began erecting tiny hills in front of them. They used stones, sticks, earth, and anything else they thought might deflect a bullet. This procedure generated discussion. Some of the men wanted to fight like duelists. They thought it right to stand tall and be a target from head to foot. They said that they scorned the devices of the cautious. The others scoffed in reply and pointed to the veterans who were digging at the ground like terriers. There soon was quite a barricade along the regimental fronts.

However, the men were ordered to withdraw from that place. This astounded Henry. "Then, why did they march us out here?" he demanded of Jim. Although Jim had been compelled to leave a little protection of stones and dirt to which he had devoted much care and skill, he calmly explained.

When the 124th was aligned in another position, each man's regard for his safety caused another line of small entrenchments. The men ate their noon meal behind a third one. They were moved from this one, too. They were marched from place to place with apparent aimlessness.

Henry was feverishly impatient. The generals seemed to lack purpose. "I can't stand this much longer," he cried out to Jim. "I don't see what good it does to make us wear out our legs for nothing." He wanted to either return to camp or go into battle and find that he was just as brave as other men.

Jim prepared a sandwich of crackers and pork and nonchalantly swallowed it. "I guess we have to reconnoiter to keep them from getting too close or something."

"Huh!" Ned scoffed.

"Well," Henry said, fidgeting, "I'd rather do almost anything than tramp around the country all day doing no good to anybody and just tiring ourselves out."

"So would I," Ned said. "It isn't right. If anybody with any sense was running this army . . ."

"Shut up, you damn fool!" Jim roared. "You haven't had that uniform on for six months, but you talk as if you know goddamn everything."

"Well, I want to do some fighting," Ned said. "I didn't come here to walk. I could have walked at home, round and round the barn."

Red-faced, Jim swallowed another sandwich as if taking poison in despair. Gradually, as he chewed, his face became quiet and content again. Whenever he ate, he seemed to blissfully contemplate his food. He accepted new environments and circumstances with great coolness, eating from his haversack at every opportunity. On the march he hadn't objected to the pace or distance. When ordered away from the three little protective piles of earth and stone that he had created, he hadn't raised his voice.

In the afternoon the 124th went out over the same ground as in the morning. The landscape no longer threatened Henry. It seemed familiar now. However, when they passed into a new area, his fear returned. At one point he concluded that it would be best to get killed. That would end his troubles.

The skirmish fire increased to a long chattering sound mingled with faraway cheering. After a time Henry saw the skirmishers running, pursued by the sound of musket fire. Then the rifles' hot, dangerous flashes were visible. Smoke clouds slowly crossed the fields. The din increased, like the roar of an approaching train.

With a rending roar, a brigade ahead of them went into action. They lay stretched in the distance behind a long gray wall of smoke.

Henry gazed spellbound, his eyes wide and his mouth slightly open. Suddenly he felt a heavy hand on his shoulder. He turned and saw Ned.

"It's my first and last battle," Ned said with intense gloom. He was pale. His girlish lips trembled.

"What?" Henry murmured in astonishment.

"It's my first and last battle. Something tells me I'm a goner. I want you to take these things to my folks." He ended in a sob of self-pity, handing Henry a small packet.

"What the devil...?" Henry began.

Ned gave him a look as if from a tomb's depths, raised his limp hand in a silencing gesture, and turned away.

CHAPTER
4

The brigade was halted at a grove's fringe. The men crouched among the trees and pointed their guns out at the fields. Beyond the smoke they saw running men, some of whom gestured and shouted information.

The men of the 124th watched and listened eagerly and discussed rumors about the battle.

"They say Perry has been driven in with big loss."

"That smart lieutenant is commanding G Company."

"Carrott went to the hospital. He said he was sick. The boys say they won't be under him anymore even if they all have to desert. They always knew he was an asshole."

"Hannisey's heavy artillery has been taken."

"No, it hasn't. I saw it over on the left not more than fifteen minutes ago. General Alston says he's going to take command of the 124th when we go into action. He says we'll fight like no other regiment ever has."

"They say we're catching it over on the left. They say the enemy drove our line into a swamp."

"That young Hasbrouck is a good officer. He isn't afraid of anything."

"I met one of the 148th Maine boys. He says his brigade fought the whole rebel army for four hours over on the turnpike and killed about five thousand of them. He says one more fight like that and the war will be over."

"Bill wasn't scared. No, sir! He just was mad. When that fellow stepped on his hand, he said that he was willing to give his hand to his country, but he'd be damned if he was going to have some dumb yokel walking around on it. Three of his fingers were crushed, so he went to the hospital. The damn doctor wanted to amputate them, and Bill raised a hell of a row."

The din in front swelled to a tremendous chorus. Henry and his fellows froze in silence. They saw a flag waving in the smoke. The blurred and agitated forms of troops were near the flag. A turbulent stream of men crossed the fields. Heavy artillery changed position at a frantic gallop, scattering the stragglers right and left.

A screaming shell went over the reserves' huddled heads. It landed in the grove and exploded, flinging earth. There a small shower of pine needles. Bullets whistled among the branches and nipped at the trees. Twigs and leaves came sailing down. Many of the men constantly dodged and ducked.

Lieutenant Hasbrouck was shot in the hand. He swore so much that a nervous laugh went along the regimental line. Hasbrouck's profanity sounded conventional, as if he had hit his fingers with a hammer at home. It relieved the new men's tension. Hasbrouck held his wounded hand away from his side so that the blood wouldn't drip onto his trousers. Tucking his sword under his arm, the company's captain produced a handkerchief and started to bind Hasbrouck's wound. They disputed how the binding should be done.

The battle flag in the distance jerked about madly. Horizontal flashes filled the billowing smoke. Running men emerged from the smoke. They grew in numbers until it was seen that the whole brigade was fleeing. The flag suddenly sank as if dying.

Wild yells came from behind the walls of smoke. A sketch in gray and red dissolved into a mob-like body of men who galloped like wild horses.

The veteran regiments on the 124th's right and left began to jeer. Loud catcalls and mocking advice concerning places to hide mingled with the sounds of bullets and shrieks of shells.

The 124th was breathless with horror. "God! Saunders's regiment got crushed!" the man at Henry's elbow whispered. The men of the 124th shrank back and crouched as if awaiting a flood.

Henry swiftly glanced along the regiment's blue ranks. The profiles were motionless. The flag bearer was standing with his legs apart, as if he expected to be pushed to the ground.

The retreating throng went whirling around the flank. Cursing, officers struck around them with their swords and left fists, punching every head they could reach. One mounted officer raged with his head, arms, and legs. Another officer, the brigade's commander, galloped around bawling. His hat was gone. His clothes were awry. His horse's hoofs often threatened the heads of the running men, who somehow escaped injury. They didn't heed the largest, longest oaths that were thrown at them from all directions. The grim jokes of the critical veterans frequently could be heard over this tumult, but the retreating men took no notice. Their bleached cheeks and wild eyes frightened Henry. The stampede exerted a flood-like force that seemed able to drag men along. The reserves had to hold firm.

During moments of waiting, Henry thought of home. He remembered a circus parade down his village's main street one spring day. A small boy, he had been thrilled by the dingy lady on a white horse and the band in a faded chariot. Henry pictured the yellow road, lines of expectant people, and sober houses. He especially remembered an old fellow who would sit on a cracker box in front of the village store and pretend to despise such exhibitions. A thousand details of form and color surged in Henry's mind.

Someone cried, "Here they come!"

The men stirred and muttered. They pulled their cartridge boxes into various positions and adjusted them with great care. Having prepared his rifle, Jim took out a red handkerchief and carefully wrapped it around his throat.

"Here they come!" was repeated up and down the line in a muffled roar. Gun locks clicked.

Yelling shrilly, stooping, and swinging their rifles at all angles, a swarm of Confederate soldiers came running across the smoke-infested fields. A flag, tilted forward, sped near the front.

As he saw the opposing forces, Henry was startled by the thought that maybe his gun wasn't loaded. He stood trying to remember the moment when he had loaded, but he couldn't.

Hatless, General Alston pulled his dripping horse to a stand near Colonel MacChesnay. Alston shook his fist in MacChesnay's face and shouted savagely, "You've got to hold them back!"

MacChesnay stammered, "All right, General. All right. We'll do our . . . We . . . we'll do our best."

Alston made a passionate gesture and galloped away.

To relieve his own feelings of frustration, MacChesnay began to scold others.

Turning swiftly to make sure that the rear was unmolested, Henry saw an officer looking at his men as if he deeply regretted his association with them.

The man at Henry's elbow was mumbling to himself, "We're in for it now. We're in for it now."

The company's captain paced excitedly in the rear. "Hold your fire, boys," he said. "Don't shoot until I tell you. Save your fire. Wait until they get close."

Perspiration streamed down Henry's face. He frequently wiped his eyes with his coat sleeve. His mouth was slightly open. He threw his rifle into position and fired a first wild shot. Then he fired automatically. He lost concern for himself. He became a part of something—a regiment, an army, a cause, a country—in crisis. He was welded into a common personality dominated by a single desire.

The regiment's noise assured Henry. The

124th wheezed and banged with a mighty power. He pictured the ground strewn with dead Confederates. He felt his comrades around him. The brotherhood of battle was even more potent than the cause for which they were fighting. There was furious haste in Henry's movements.

Presently Henry began to feel the effects of the war atmosphere: a blistering sweat, a sensation that his eyeballs were about to crack like parched earth. A burning roar filled his ears. A red rage followed. He developed the sharp exasperation of a tormented animal, such as a cow nipped at by dogs. He felt anger toward his rifle because it could fire at only one person at a time. He wanted to rush forward and strangle people. His impotency enraged him as if he were a driven beast. Buried in the smoke of many rifles, he fought frantically for air.

On all faces hot rage mingled with intentness. Many of the men muttered curses, prayers, encouragement, or insults, and this muttering created a strange, chant-like undercurrent. The man at Henry's elbow was babbling. Jim was swearing loudly. Another complained, "Why don't they support us? Why don't they send supports?"

There were no heroic poses. In their haste and rage, the men bent and surged. Their steel ramrods clanked as they pounded them into hot rifle barrels. The flaps of their cartridge boxes were unfastened; they bobbed idiotically with each movement. The men jerked their rifles to their shoulders and fired without apparent aim into the smoke or at one of the blurry, shifting forms that had been growing larger in the field before them.

The officers, too, showed no picturesque attitudes. They bobbed to and fro, roaring instructions and encouragement.

Hasbrouck encountered a soldier who had fled, screaming, at his comrades' first volley. These two were acting out a small, isolated scene behind the lines. The man was blubbering and staring with sheep-like eyes at Hasbrouck, who had seized him by the collar and was pummeling him. With many blows Hasbrouck drove him back into the ranks. The soldier went mechanically, dully, with his eyes on Hasbrouck. He tried to reload his gun, but his hands were shaking too much. Hasbrouck assisted him.

The men dropped here and there like bundles. The captain of Henry's company was killed. His body lay stretched out in the position of a tired man resting. His face had a sorrowful, astonished look, as if he thought some friend had done him an ill turn.

The babbling man was grazed by a shot that made blood stream down his face. He clapped both hands to his head, cried "Oh!" and ran.

Another man suddenly grunted as if he had been struck by a club in the stomach. He sat down and gazed sorrowfully and reproachfully.

Farther up the line a ball splintered the kneecap of a man who was standing behind a tree. He immediately dropped his rifle and gripped the tree with both arms. He remained there, clinging desperately and crying for assistance.

At last an exultant yell went along the quivering line. The firing dwindled from an uproar to a last vindictive popping. As the smoke slowly cleared, Henry saw that the charge had been repulsed. The Confederates were scattered into reluctant groups. He saw a man climb to the top of a fence, straddle it, and fire a parting shot.

Some in the 124th began to whoop. Many were silent. After the fever left his veins, Henry thought he was going to suffocate. He became aware of the foul atmosphere. He was grimy and dripping. He grasped his canteen and took a long swallow of the warm water.

Up and down the line, men said, "We've held them back. We've held them back." They said it blissfully, leering at one another with dirty smiles.

Henry looked behind him, to the right, and to the left. Corpses lay twisted in fantastic contortions. Arms were bent and heads were turned in incredible ways.

From a position in the rear, a row of heavy artillery threw shells over the grove. At first the guns' flash startled Henry, who thought the guns were aimed at him. Through the trees he watched the gunners as they worked swiftly and intently. He wondered how they could remember what to do amid such confusion.

A small procession of wounded men went drearily toward the rear. To the right and left were the dark lines of other troops. Here and there were Union flags, like beautiful birds undaunted in a storm. Henry felt the old thrill at the sight of the emblem. A deep, pulsating thunder came from far to the left. Lesser clamors came from many directions. It occurred to Henry that men were fighting over there, and over there, and over there. Previously he had supposed that all of the fighting was directly under his nose.

As he gazed around him, Henry was astonished by the blue, pure sky and the sunlight gleaming on trees and fields. It was surprising that nature had tranquilly continued amid so much deviltry.

"At last it's over," Henry thought. He had passed the supreme trial. He felt an ecstasy of self-satisfaction. He considered himself a fine fellow. He beamed tenderness and good will toward his fellows. "Boy, it's hot today, huh?" he said in a friendly way to another soldier.

"You bet," the man answered, grinning sociably. "I've never known such heat." He sprawled luxuriously on the ground. "And I hope we don't have any more fighting for a while."

Henry shook hands and spoke with men whose features were familiar but with whom he now felt the bonds of tied hearts for the first time. He helped a cursing comrade bind a shin wound.

Suddenly cries of amazement broke out along the 124th's ranks. "Here they come again!"

The man who had sprawled on the ground started up. "God!"

Henry quickly looked at the field. He saw forms emerging from a distant wood and a tilted flag speeding forward. The shells, which had ceased to trouble the regiment for a time, came swirling again, exploding in the grass and among the leaves of trees.

The men groaned. The luster faded from their eyes. Their dirty faces showed profound dejection. They slowly moved their stiff bodies and sullenly watched the Confederates' frantic approach. They complained, "This is too much. Why can't somebody send us supports?"

"We'll never survive this second banging. I didn't come here to fight the whole damn rebel army."

One man whined, "I wish Bill Smithers had stepped on *my* hand instead of me stepping on *his*."

Henry stared. Surely this impossible thing wasn't about to happen. He waited as if he expected the Confederates to stop, apologize, and go away. But the firing began somewhere on the regimental line and ripped along in both directions. The level sheets of flame developed great smoke clouds that rolled through the ranks. The flag sometimes disappeared in this vapor, but more often it projected, sun-touched and resplendent.

The look in Henry's eyes resembled the look in the eyes of worn-out horses. His neck quivered with nervous weakness; his arms seemed to go numb; his hands seemed large and awkward as if he were wearing mittens; his knees were unsteady. Exhausted, he was amazed by the Confederates' endurance. They must be steel machines. He slowly lifted his rifle and fired at a cantering cluster. Then he stopped and looked through the smoke. The ground was covered with running, yelling men. Henry was horrified.

A nearby man who had been feverishly working at his rifle suddenly stopped and ran, howling. A lad whose face had previously borne an expression of exalted courage was smitten with terror. He paled, threw down his gun, and fled. There was no shame in his face. He ran like a rabbit. Others began to run away through the smoke.

Henry turned his head and saw the fleeing forms. He yelled with fright, swung around, and began to speed toward the rear. His rifle and cap were gone. His unbuttoned coat bulged in the wind. The flap of his cartridge box bobbed wildly. His canteen swung out behind on its slender cord.

Henry saw Hasbrouck spring forward, yelling and red-faced, and jab with his sword.

Henry ran so blindly that he fell down several times. Once he knocked his shoulder against a tree so violently that he went headlong. He dimly saw men on his right and left. He heard footsteps behind him. This comforted him. Being closer to the Confederates, the men behind him would be killed before *he* would. He made an effort not to be outraced.

Leading, he crossed a small field as shells hurtled over his head with long, wild screams. One exploded in front of him. He groveled on the ground and then, springing up, went careering off through some bushes. He was amazed when he came within view of Union artillery. The men operating it seemed unaware of impending annihilation. The gunners seemed cool and precise. Henry pitied them as he ran. "Idiots!" he thought. "Planting shells will do them little good when the enemy comes swooping out of the woods."

Henry saw a brigade going to the relief of its hard-pressed fellows. He scrambled up a small hill and watched the brigade sweep in, keeping its formation even in difficult places. Brilliant flags projected from the line of blue. Officers were shouting. One, on a bounding horse, made maniacal arm movements.

Henry went on at a less frantic pace. He came upon a general on a horse whose ears were pricked with interest in the battle. The saddle and bridle gleamed with yellow and patent leather. Jingling staff galloped here and there. Sometimes the general was surrounded by horsemen; at other times he was alone.

Henry slinked around, going as near as he dared in an attempt to overhear words. He felt a desire to thrash the general or at least tell him what a fool he was. It was criminal to stay calmly in one spot and make no effort to stop destruction.

The general called out irritably, "Tompkins, go over and see Taylor. Tell him to halt his brigade at the edge of the woods. Tell him to detach a regiment. Say that I think the center will break if we don't help it out. Tell him to hurry."

A slim youth on a fine chestnut horse, Tompkins galloped off in a cloud of dust.

A moment later the general bounced excitedly in his saddle. "By heaven, they've held them back! Yes, they have! They've held them!" His face was aflame with excitement. He happily roared at his staff, "We'll wallop them now. We'll wallop them!" He turned to an aid. "Jones. Quick. Go to Taylor. Tell him to go in like blazes."

As Jones galloped off, the general beamed like the sun. He kept repeating, "They've held them, by heaven!"

Henry cringed as if discovered in a crime. They had won! The 124th had stood fast and triumphed! He could hear cheering. He stood on his toes and looked in the direction of the fight. A yellow fog veiled the treetops. Musketry clattered. Hoarse cries indicated an advance. Henry turned away, angry and amazed. He felt he had been wronged. Annihilation had seemed certain.

Henry told himself that in saving himself he had saved a piece of the army. Unless many people acted as he did, there wouldn't be an army. He had acted wisely and out of righteous motives. But he started to wonder what his fellows would say when he appeared in camp. They would deride him. He began to pity himself.

Shambling along with bowed head, he went from the fields into thick woods. He wanted to get out of hearing of the crackling shots, which seemed like voices. The ground was cluttered with vines, bushes, and saplings. He couldn't make his way without making swishing and cracking noises. He feared that the noises might attract attention, so he sought dark places that would conceal him.

After a time the sound of musketry grew faint; the cannon boomed in the distance. Suddenly the sun blazed among the trees. Insects made rhythmical noises. A woodpecker stuck her head around the side of a tree. A bird flew on lighthearted wing. The scene reassured him. The religion of peace.

Henry threw a pine cone at a squirrel, who ran. The squirrel stopped high in a treetop and, poking his head from behind a branch, cautiously looked down. This, too, reassured Henry. Recognizing danger, the squirrel had run. He hadn't stood facing the missile, waiting to die. He had fled. Henry had done the same. It was only natural to seek safety.

At length Henry reached a place where high, arching boughs formed a chapel. He softly pushed the boughs aside and entered. Pine needles provided a gentle brown carpet. There was a religious half-light. He stopped near the threshold, horror-stricken. A dead man was looking at him. In a uniform faded from blue to green, the corpse sat with its back against a tree. The eyes were glazed over. The mouth was open; its red had changed to an appalling yellow. Black ants swarmed over the face's gray skin; one of them carried some sort of bundle along the upper lip. Henry shrieked and turned to stone. Then he retreated, step by step, with his eyes on the corpse. He feared that if he turned his back, the body might spring up and pursue him. When the corpse was out of sight, he turned and fled.

CHAPTER
5

The trees began to sing a soft hymn of twilight. The sun sank until slanted bronze rays struck the forest. There was a lull in the noises of insects as if they had stopped to bow their heads in silent prayer.

Suddenly a tremendous clangor broke upon this stillness. Musketry and artillery clattered, crackled, and thundered from the distance. Henry began to run toward the battle. He wanted to peer out from the forest's edge. Soon he could see long, gray walls of vapor: battle lines. Cannon shots shook him. Musketry sounded in long, irregular surges. He went closer. The battle's complexity and grim power fascinated him. He wanted to see the battle produce corpses.

Henry came to a fence and clambered over. On the far side clothes and guns littered the ground. A folded newspaper lay in the dirt. A dead soldier was stretched with his face hidden in his arm. Farther off was a group of five corpses putrid from the hot sun. Henry hurried on, slightly fearful that one of the swollen forms would rise up and speak to him.

Finally Henry came to a road streaming with wounded men, who cursed, groaned, and wailed. The earth-swaying sound of musketry and artillery, mingled with cheers, always was in the air. The steady current of maimed men came from the region of the noises.

One wounded man hopped on one leg. His other leg streamed blood. He laughed hysterically. Another was swearing that he'd been shot in the arm through General Hooker's mismanagement of the army. With a look of agony, another man sang, "Five and twenty dead men baked in a pie." Parts of the procession limped and staggered in rhythm with his tune.

Two privates carried an officer, who cried, "Don't joggle me so, Johnson! Do you think my leg is made of iron? If you can't carry me decently, put me down and let someone else do it." The officer bellowed at the tottering crowd, who blocked his bearers' quick march. "Make way, can't you? Make way, damn it!" The men sulkily parted and went to the roadsides. As the officer was carried past, they made insulting remarks to him. When he raged in reply and threatened them, they told him to be damned.

cried out, "I'll take care of you, Jim!
re of you! I swear to God!"
you, Henry?" Jim begged.
es. I'll take care of you!"

m continued to beg. He clung to
m. His eyes rolled in terror. "I was
ood friend to you, wasn't I, Henry?
been a pretty good fellow, haven't I?
ne out of the road, so the artillery
ne over. Just pull me out of the road.
for you. You know I would." He
aiting Henry's reply.

started to sob.

ly Jim seemed to forget his fears. He
forward. Henry wanted Jim to lean
ut Jim always shook his head and
rotested, "No, leave me alone." Jim
i to stare into nothingness.

heard a soft voice near his shoulders.
saw Dave. "You'd better take him
oad," Dave said. "Artillery is coming
ad. He'll get run over. He'll be dead
tes anyway. You can see that. You'd
him out of the road."

grasped Jim by the arm. "Jim," he
ne with me."

kly tried to wrench himself free. He
nry for a moment. Then he asked,
elds?" He started blindly through

Henry joined this crowd and marched along with it. The torn bodies indicated the awful machinery in which the men had been entangled. Orderlies and couriers occasionally galloped through the roadway crowd, scattering wounded men right and left. Sometimes artillery came thumping down on the men, the officers shouting orders to clear the way.

A tattered man fouled with dust, blood, and powder stain from hair to shoes trudged along, eagerly listening to a bearded sergeant's lurid descriptions. His lean features expressed awe and admiration. His mouth was agape. The sergeant paused in his descriptions to mock the tattered man: "Be careful, or you'll be attracting flies." Taken aback, the tattered man shrank back.

After a time the tattered man came up to Henry. His voice was as gentle as a girl's; his eyes were pleading. He had a head wound bound with a blood-soaked rag. His arm dangled like a broken branch. "Hi. I'm Dave. It was a pretty good fight, wasn't it?" he timidly said to Henry.

"Yes," Henry said with annoyance. He quickened his pace.

Needing to talk, Dave hobbled after him. With an apologetic tone, he repeated, "It was a pretty good fight. I've never seen fellows fight like that. I knew the boys would fight like that when they got the chance. This time they showed the Johnnies what's what. I knew it would turn out this way. You can't lick those boys. No, sir. They're fighters." He took a deep breath of humble admiration and looked at Henry for encouragement. Although he didn't receive any, he went on. "They fought and fought. No matter how bad it got, they didn't run." Dave's homely face was suffused with a light of love for the army. In a brotherly tone he asked Henry, "Where were you hit?"

Henry felt panic. "What?"

"Where were you hit?"

"I . . . I . . . " Henry turned away and slid through the crowd. His brow was heavily flushed. His fingers picked nervously at one of his buttons. He bent his head and fastened his eyes on the button.

Dave looked after him in astonishment.

Henry fell back in the procession until Dave was out of sight. Then he walked on with the others. But he was amid the wounded. Because of Dave's question, he now felt that his shame was visible. He continually cast sidelong glances to see if men were contemplating the letters of guilt he felt were burned into his brow.

At times Henry regarded the wounded soldiers with envy. He wished that he too had a wound, a red badge of courage.

Another soldie
side. When he turn
started as if bitter
Jim!"

Jim walked sti
hard lines; his tee
were bloody from
Death's seal alread
gray and waxen. J
way. "Hello, Hen

Henry tottere
"Oh . . . Jim . . .

"Where have
you were killed.
today."

Henry still la

"I was out
monotonous tor
shot." He seeme
know how this c

Henry put
Jim walked on
seemed overco
Henry's arm an
ing to be overh
whisper, "I'll tel
I'm afraid I'll
artillery wagons
I'm afraid of."

Henry
I'll take ca
"Will
"Yes.
But Ji
Henry's a
always a g
I've always
Just pull
can't run
I'd do tha
paused, aw

Henry
Sudden
went stonil
on him, b
strangely p
now seeme

Henry
Turning, h
out of the r
down the ro
in five minu
better take

Henry
coaxed, "co
Jim wea
stared at H
"Into the fi

the grass.

Henry turned to look at the lashing riders and jouncing artillery. He was startled from this view by a shrill outcry from Dave: "God! He's running!"

Turning his head swiftly, Henry saw Jim running in a staggering, stumbling way toward a clump of bushes. The sight squeezed his heart. He and Dave began a pursuit.

When Henry overtook Jim, he pleaded, "Jim, Jim. What are you doing? You'll hurt yourself."

"No. Don't touch me," Jim answered. "Leave me alone."

"Where are you going, Jim? What are you doing?" Henry persisted.

There was a great appeal in Jim's eyes. "Can't you leave me alone?" Jim turned and, lurching dangerously, went on.

Henry and Dave followed but hung back a bit, awed and afraid. At last Jim stopped and stood motionless. Hurrying up to him, Henry and Dave saw from his face that he had found what he was looking for. His bloody hands were quietly at his side. He waited patiently. Henry and Dave paused and stood, expectant.

Finally, Jim's chest began to heave. The heaving became more violent. Jim's eyes rolled. He stiffened and straightened, then shook. He stared into space. For a moment leg tremors caused him to dance a hideous hornpipe. His arms beat wildly about his head as if in enthusiasm. He stretched himself to his full height. There was a slight rending sound. Then he began to swing forward, slow and straight, like a falling tree. A swift muscular contortion made his left shoulder strike the ground first. His body seemed to bounce a little.

"God!" Dave said.

Henry had watched in anguish. He now went up close to Jim and gazed at his face. The mouth was open; the teeth showed in a laugh. The flap of Jim's blue jacket fell away from the body. Jim's side looked as if wolves had chewed it. Henry turned toward the battlefield with sudden rage. He shook his fist and cried, "Hell!"

The red sun was pasted in the sky like a wafer.

Dave stood thinking. Finally he said in an awestruck voice, "Wow. I've never seen such strength and nerve." He poked one of Jim's lifeless hands with his foot. "I wonder where he got his strength. I've never seen a man do anything like this before. Wow."

Henry wanted to screech with grief, but his tongue lay dead in his mouth. He threw himself onto the ground.

After a time, while looking at the corpse, Dave said, "Look here. He's dead and gone, so we might as well begin to look out for number one. This thing is over. He's dead and gone, and he's all right here. Nobody will bother him. I'm not in the best health myself right now."

Henry looked up and saw that Dave was swinging uncertainly on his legs. His face had turned blue. "Good Lord! You aren't going to . . ."

Dave waved his hand. "I'm not dying," he said. "I just need some food and a good bed. I want pea soup. Pea soup," he repeated dreamily.

Henry got up. He and Dave gazed for a moment at the corpse. Then they turned their backs on it and started away.

"I'm starting to feel really bad," Dave said.

Henry groaned.

"Oh, I'm not planning to die just yet. I can't. I have too many children." Dave smiled weakly. "If I did die, I wouldn't do it the way that fellow did. That's the damnedest thing I ever saw. I'd just flop down. I've never seen anyone die the way that fellow did. Tom Jamison lives next door to me back home. He's a nice guy. Smart, too. He and I always were friends. When we were fighting this afternoon, all of a sudden he bellowed at me, 'You're shot! You're shot, damn it!' I looked at my fingers and saw that, sure enough, I was shot. I gave a holler and started to run, but before I could get away, I was shot in the arm. It whirled me clean around. I got scared and ran like hell. So I've been shot two places, and I'm really starting to feel it now. I don't think I can walk much farther."

Henry and Dave went on slowly in silence. "You look pretty sick yourself," Dave resumed. "Your wound might be worse than you think. You'd better take care of it. It might be mostly inside, and those can be the worst. Where is it?" But he continued without waiting for a reply. "I once saw a guy get hit right in the head when my regiment was standing at ease. Everybody yelled to him, 'Are you hurt, John? Are you hurt much?' He said, 'No' and looked surprised. He said he didn't feel anything. But, by God, the first thing we knew, he was dead. So, you have to watch out. You might have some weird kind of wound yourself. You never can tell. Where's your wound?"

Henry had been wriggling since the introduction of this topic. He now made an angry motion with his hand and cried, "Don't bother me!" He was enraged at Dave and could have strangled him. He turned toward Dave and repeated, "Don't bother me," with a tone of threat.

"Lord knows, I don't want to bother anybody," Dave said with some despair. "I've got enough of my own to attend to."

Looking at Dave with hatred, Henry harshly said, "Goodbye."

Dave looked at him in gaping amazement. "Why, where are you going?" he asked unsteadily. Then he started to be delirious. "Now look here, Tom Jamison. I won't have this. It won't do. Where are you going?"

Henry pointed vaguely. "Over there."

"Now look here," Dave rambled on. His head hung forward, and his words were slurred. "You need me to take care of you, Tom. You can't go traipsing off with a bad hurt."

Henry climbed a fence and started away. He could hear Dave pleading, but he went on. Glancing back from a distance, he saw Dave wandering helplessly in the field.

Henry wished he were dead. He envied the men whose bodies lay strewn over the fields' grass and the forest's fallen leaves. Dave's simple question had been a knife thrust to him. Dave's persistence made him feel that he wouldn't be able to keep his crime concealed.

CHAPTER 6

The battle's furnace roar was growing louder. Great brown clouds floated before Henry. The fields became dotted with men. Henry rounded a hillock and saw that the roadway now was a mass of wagons, horses, and men. Urgings, curses, and commands issued from the heaving tangle. Fear swept all of it along. Whips cracked and bit; horses plunged and tugged. The white-topped wagons strained and stumbled.

This sight comforted Henry. Everyone was retreating. Maybe he wasn't so bad, then. He seated himself and watched the terror-stricken people driving the wagons. Their roaring, cursing, and lashing assured him that he had been justified in fleeing the battlefield's dangers and horrors.

A column of infantry appeared in the road. It came swiftly on, moving in a serpentine way to avoid obstructions. The men prodded teamsters and butted mules with their muskets. They made their way through the dense mass by sheer force. Commands to "Make way!" had a ring of importance. Going forward to confront the Confederates, the men were proud of their onward movement. They tumbled teams about with indifference, caring only that they should reach the front in time. This importance made their faces grave and stern. The officers' backs were rigid.

As Henry looked at the men, the black weight of his woe returned. The forward-going soldiers seemed to march with weapons of flame and banners of sunlight. He never could be like them. He wanted to weep. He blamed some indefinite cause, not himself. Then he imagined himself one of the men. Holding a broken blade high, standing with determination before a crimson and steel assault, he would lead a charge. Before everyone's eyes he calmly would get killed. His dead body would be magnificent in its pathos. These thoughts uplifted him. He soared on war's red wings.

Henry considered joining the column. He had no rifle, but rifles could be had for the picking; they were all around. He wouldn't be able to find his regiment, but he could fight with any regiment. He started forward slowly. What if comrades of his spotted him returning this way? They'd know that he had fled. He decided not to go.

Henry realized that he had a scorching thirst. His face was so dry that he thought he could feel his skin crackle. Every bone of his body seemed to ache and threaten to break at any movement. His feet were like two sores. Also, his body was calling for food. When he tried to walk, his head swayed and he tottered. Small patches of green mist floated before his vision.

Henry stayed near the battle. He wanted to see what was happening and get news. He wanted to know who was winning. He knew that defeat would be good for him. It would splinter regiments. Many brave men would be separated from their comrades. He would seem to be one of them. In contrast, if the army was victorious, he would be doomed to contempt and isolation. If the men were advancing, their feet were trampling his chances of a happy life.

Then the selfishness of his thoughts increased his feelings of guilt. He pictured the defiant soldiers who would place their bodies before the Confederates' bayonets and imagined their dripping corpses. He thought of himself as their murderer.

What would he tell his comrades? He considered many different lies, but he saw holes in all of them. He imagined the whole 124th saying, "Where's Henry Fleming? He ran, didn't he?"

The column that had stoutly butted against

the roadway's obstacles barely was out of sight before Henry saw dark waves of men sweep out of the woods and down through the fields. He immediately knew that the steel fibers had been washed from their hearts. They were bursting from their coats and equipment as from entanglements. They charged down on him like terrified buffaloes. Behind them blue smoke curled above the treetops. Sometimes Henry could see a distant pink glare through the thickets. The cannons clamored.

Henry stared in horror. He forgot his own mental struggle. The fight was lost. War, the red animal, the blood-swollen god, would be filled to bloating. Soon Henry was amid the fleeing men. Their pale faces shone in the dusk. Sometimes they talked incoherently. Weeping in pain and dismay, one large man asked the sky, "Where's the plank road? Where's the plank road?" Men ran every which way. Artillery boomed before, behind, to the left, and to the right, destroying a sense of direction. Landmarks vanished in the increasing gloom. The men asked a thousand wild questions, but no one answered.

Henry rushed around, throwing questions at the retreating infantry. Clutching a man by the arm, he asked, "What happened? What happened?"

The man screamed, "Let go of me!" His face was livid. He was heaving and panting. He still grasped his rifle. He tugged frantically. "Let go!"

The man fiercely swung his rifle and bashed Henry on the head. Then he ran on.

Lightning flashed before Henry's vision. A deafening rumble thundered within his head. Henry sank to the ground, struggled to rise, managed to get halfway up, then fell again. His face was pale. He groaned. At last, with a twisting movement he got onto his hands and knees and then to his feet. Pressing his hands to his temples, he lurched over the grass. He fought against fainting. He fearfully put his hand to the top of his head and touched the wound. The pain of contact made him draw a long breath through his clenched teeth. His fingers were dabbled with blood. He stared at them.

Around him Henry heard the rumble of jolted cannons as horses were lashed toward the front. One young officer on a charger nearly ran him down. Henry turned and watched the mass of guns, men, and horses sweeping in a wide curve toward a gap in a fence. The officer was gesturing excitedly with a gloved hand.

Some officers of the scattered infantry were cursing and railing. Henry heard their scolding voices above the din. A cavalry squadron rode into the jumble in the roadway. Their uniforms' faded yellow trim shone bravely.

Evening's blue haze was upon the field. The lines of forest were long purple shadows. One cloud lay along the western sky partly smothering sunset's red.

As Henry left the scene behind him, he heard the guns suddenly roar. He hurried on in the dusk. The purple darkness was filled with jabbering men. Sometimes Henry saw them gesticulating against the sky. A multitude of men and munitions was spread about in the forest and fields.

The narrow roadway now lay lifeless. There were overturned wagons, horses' bodies, and splintered parts of war machines.

Henry's wound now caused him little pain. Instead it felt cool and liquid. He imagined blood moving slowly down under his hair. His head seemed swollen. This frightened him. Suddenly he thought about home. He remembered meals that included his favorite foods. He saw the spread table. The kitchen's pine walls glowed in the stove's warm light. He also remembered how he and schoolmates would go from the schoolhouse to a shaded pool. He saw his clothes heaped on the pool's grassy bank and felt the fragrant water on his body. The leaves of the overhanging maple rustled in the summer wind.

A dragging weariness soon overcame Henry.

His head hung forward. His shoulders stooped as if he were bearing a great bundle. His feet shuffled.

At last he heard a cheerful voice near his shoulder. "You seem to be in pretty bad shape, boy."

Without looking up, Henry gave a thick-tongued "Uh" of agreement.

The man laughed and took Henry firmly by the arm. "I'm going your way. The whole gang is. I'll help you along. I'm George. What's your name?"

"Henry."

They began to walk like a drunken man and his friend.

"Which regiment do you belong to?" George asked.

"The 124th New York," Henry answered.

"I guess nearly everybody got their share of fighting today. I gave myself up for dead any number of times. There was so much shooting and hollering in the damn darkness that I hardly could tell which side I was on. Everything's a mess. It'll be a miracle if we find our regiments tonight. How did you get way over here, anyhow? The 124th is a long way from here, isn't it? Well, I guess we can find it. Today a boy I really liked was killed. Jack was a nice fellow, a sergeant. He was standing still when a big, fat guy poked at his elbow and asked, 'Where's the road to the river?' Jack didn't pay any attention. He just kept looking ahead trying to see the Johnnies coming through the woods. The fat guy kept poking at Jack's elbow, asking, 'Where's the road to the river?' Finally Jack turned around and said, 'Go to hell!' Just then a shot slapped him bang on the side of his head. Those were his last words: 'Go to hell.' I wish we were sure of finding our regiments tonight. It's going to be hard, but I guess we can do it."

In the search that followed, George's ability to thread his way through mazes of tangled forest amazed Henry. The forest seemed a vast hive of men buzzing in frantic circles, but George conducted Henry without mistakes. Finally George chuckled with glee and self-satisfaction and said, "There you are. See that fire?"

Henry nodded stupidly.

"That's your regiment. Goodbye now, and good luck to you."

George's warm, strong hand briefly clasped Henry's limp fingers. Then, with cheerful and bold whistling, George strode away. Only then it occurred to Henry that he hadn't even seen George's face.

CHAPTER
7

Henry headed slowly toward the campfires. The ground was strewn with sleeping men. Suddenly Henry confronted a black, monstrous figure. A rifle barrel glinted. "Halt! Halt!"

Henry recognized the nervous voice. Tottering before the rifle barrel, Henry said, "Is that you, Wilson?"

The rifle was lowered, and Ned slowly came forward. "Is that you, Henry?"

"Yes."

"Well, by God, I'm glad to see you. I thought you must be dead." There was husky emotion in Ned's voice.

Henry found that he barely could stand. He staggered. "I got shot," he said, so that no one would know he had run from battle. "I got shot in the head and got separated from the regiment. I don't know how."

Ned stepped forward quickly. "Shot? Why didn't you say so right away? Hold on a minute. I'll call Simpson."

At that moment Corporal Simpson loomed out of the gloom. "Who are you talking to, Wilson?" he demanded angrily. "You're the damnedest guard. Why . . . hello, Henry. Is that you? I thought you were dead. Men keep turning up every ten minutes! We thought we'd lost forty-two men, but if they keep coming at this rate, we'll have most of the company back by morning. Where were you?"

"Over on the right. I got separated," Henry began.

Ned hastily said, "He got shot in the head. We have to see to him right away." He rested his rifle in the hollow of his left arm and put his right arm around Henry's shoulder. "It must hurt bad."

Henry leaned heavily on Ned. "Yes, it hurts." His voice faltered.

Simpson linked his arm in Henry's and drew him forward. "Come on, Henry. I'll take care of you."

Ned called after them. "Put him to sleep in my blanket, Simpson. And . . . Hold on a minute. Here's my canteen. It's full of coffee. Look at his head by the fire. Maybe it's pretty bad. When my replacement comes in a couple of minutes, I'll be over and see to him."

Henry's senses were so deadened that Ned's voice sounded far away and he scarcely could feel the pressure of Simpson's arm. His head hung forward. His knees wobbled. Simpson led him into the fire's glare. "Now, Henry," he said, "let's look at your head."

Henry obediently sat down. Laying his rifle aside, Simpson began to fumble in Henry's bushy hair. He turned Henry's head so that the firelight beamed on it. When his fingers made contact with the wound, he said, "Here it is. Just as I thought. A ball has grazed you. You have a lump as if someone clubbed you. It stopped bleeding a long time ago. In the morning your head will be much more swollen, and it'll feel hot. Still, it's just a damn good wallop on the head—nothing more. Sit here and don't move while I get Wilson's replacement. I'll send Wilson to take care of you."

Simpson left. Henry remained on the ground, staring vacantly into the fire. After a time the things around him began to take form. In the deep shadows men sprawled in every conceivable posture. Glancing narrowly into the more distant darkness, Henry caught occasional glimpses of pale, tired faces. On the other side of the fire he observed an officer asleep, seated bolt upright with his back against a tree. Possibly disturbed by dreams, the officer swayed with little bounces and starts. His face was dusty and stained. His lower jaw hung loosely, as if too weak to assume its normal position. His sword lay on the ground.

Within the rose and orange light from the burning sticks, other soldiers snored and heaved or lay in deathlike slumber. A few pairs of legs stuck forth, rigid and straight. Their shoes displayed the mud or dust of marches; protruding from the blankets, bits of trousers showed tears from hurried movement through dense brambles. Light smoke swelled from the crackling fire. Overhead the leaves moved softly. Far off to the right, a handful of stars glittered through a window in the forest. Occasionally a soldier would turn his body to a new position or sit up, blink dumbly at the fire for a moment, quickly glance at a prostrate companion, and then cuddle down again with a grunt of sleepy content.

Henry sat in a forlorn heap until Ned came, swinging two canteens by their light strings. "Well now, Henry," Ned said. "We'll have you fixed up in about a minute." Ned had the bustling ways of an amateur nurse. He fussed around the fire and stirred the sticks. He made his patient drink coffee from the canteen.

Henry found the coffee delicious. He tilted his head far back and held the canteen to his lips for a long time. The cool mixture went caressingly down his blistered throat. When he finished, he sighed with comfort.

Ned watched Henry with satisfaction. He took a large handkerchief from his pocket, folded it into a bandage, soused its middle with water from the second canteen, and bound it over Henry's head, tying the ends in a knot at the back of Henry's neck. "There," Ned said, surveying his work. "You look like the devil, but I bet you feel better."

Henry looked gratefully at Ned. The cold cloth felt like a woman's tender hand on his aching, swelling head.

"You haven't hollered or complained, Henry. You're a good man. Most men would have been in the hospital long ago. A shot in the head isn't a light matter."

Henry didn't reply. He began to fumble with the buttons of his jacket.

"Well, we need to get you to bed now," Ned said. "You need a good night's rest."

Henry carefully stood, and Ned led him among the sleeping forms lying in groups and rows. Presently Ned stooped and picked up his blankets. He spread the rubber one on the ground and placed the woolen one around Henry's shoulders. "There," Ned said. "Lie down and get some sleep."

Henry got down and stretched out with a murmur of relief and comfort. Suddenly he cried out, "Hold on a minute! Where will *you* sleep?"

Ned waved his hand impatiently. "Beside you."

"But what are you going to sleep in? I've got your . . . "

"Shut up and go to sleep," Ned said sternly.

Henry said no more. An exquisite drowsiness spread through him. The blanket enveloped him with warm comfort. His head fell forward on his crooked arm, and his weighted lids went softly down over his eyes. Hearing a splatter of musketry from the distance, he wondered indifferently if those men sometimes slept. He gave a long sigh, snuggled down into his blanket, and in a moment was asleep.

CHAPTER
8

Henry awoke at dawn, feeling as if he'd slept a thousand years. An icy dew had chilled his face. He curled farther down into his blanket. The distance blared with fighting. When Henry looked around at the men sleeping in rows and groups, he sat up with a little cry. The grayish light gave their gaunt, careworn features a corpselike hue. For a moment he thought they all were dead.

A fire crackled briskly in the cold air. Turning his head, Henry saw Ned busily tending to a small blaze. A few other figures moved in the fog. Henry heard the cracking of ax blows.

Suddenly there was a hollow rumble of drums. A distant bugle sang faintly. Similar sounds came from near and far over the forest. The men rustled, lifted their heads, and grumbled. An officer's high voice rang out, and the men's stiff movements quickened.

Henry yawned and rubbed his eyes. "Thunder!" he complained. He carefully felt his bandage.

Ned came over from the fire. "How do you feel?"

Henry puckered his mouth. His head hurt and stomach grumbled. "Pretty bad."

"Oh," Ned said, disappointed. "I was hoping you'd feel all right this morning. Let's see the bandage. It slipped." He clumsily tinkered with the bandage.

"God damn it!" Henry exploded. "Can't you be more gentle?"

Ned answered soothingly, "Come get some food."

At the fireside Ned dipped a tin cup into an iron-colored mixture in a small tin pail and gave the cup to Henry. Ned hurriedly roasted some meat on a stick. Then he sat down and happily watched Henry devour the food.

Henry noticed that Ned had changed. Instead of being irritable and resentful, he seemed self-reliant and quietly confident. Previously Henry had regarded Ned as childish, blustering, and jealous: a swaggering babe. Now Ned seemed humble and thoughtful.

Ned balanced his coffee cup on his knee. "Well, Henry, what do you think the chances are? Do you think we'll wallop them? All the officers say we've got the rebels in a pretty tight box."

"I don't know," Henry said. "From what I saw, we got a pretty good pounding yesterday."

"You think so? I thought it was the other way around."

"Jim Conklin's dead."

Ned started. "Is he? Jim Conklin?"

"Yes. He was shot in the side."

"Poor cuss."

All around them were other small fires surrounded by men with their little tin utensils. Sharp voices suddenly came from nearby. Two soldiers had teased a huge bearded man, causing him to spill coffee on his knees. The man had gone into a rage and cursed at the two, who had bristled with indignation. A fight threatened.

Ned got up and went over to them. "Come on, boys. What's the use of fighting? We'll be at the rebels in less than a hour. What's the good of fighting among ourselves?"

One of the smaller soldiers turned on Ned with a red face. "Mind your own business." But the desire to deal blows had passed. Ned returned to his seat.

"I hate to see the boys fighting among themselves," Ned said to Henry.

Henry laughed. "You've changed. You used to pick fights, not prevent them."

"That's true," Ned said. After a thoughtful pause, he continued. "Yesterday I thought half the men in our regiment were dead, but most of them have come back. They were scattered all over, wandering in the woods, fighting with other regiments, and everything. Just like you."

CHAPTER
9

The 124th stood at arms, waiting for the command to march. Henry suddenly remembered the small packet of letters that Ned had solemnly entrusted to him. "Wilson!" he exclaimed, turning to Ned, who was at his side.

"What?"

Henry decided to avoid the topic. "Never mind."

"What were you going to say?"

"Never mind." Henry remembered how Ned had spoken, with a sob, of his own death. He would remind Ned of this if Ned ever suspected him of cowardice. For now, though, Henry felt confident and unashamed. No one had discovered his fleeing. He had made his mistakes in the dark, so he still was a man. He told himself that a man respected by his fellows has no reason to scold himself. In fact, his escaping both death and punishment gave him new confidence.

that he had heard going from group to group at the camp that morning. "The brigadier said he never saw a new regiment fight the way we did yesterday. And we didn't do better than many other regiments, did we? Well, then you can't say it's the army's fault, can you?"

Ned's voice was stern. "Of course not. No man dare say that we don't fight like the devil. But that doesn't mean we always can win."

"If we fight like the devil but don't win, it must be Alston's fault," Henry said. "I don't see any point in fighting and fighting but losing because of some lunkhead general."

A man tramping at Henry's side said sarcastically, "Maybe you think you fought the whole battle yesterday, Fleming."

Henry was alarmed. Had this man seen him run? "No, I don't think I fought the whole battle," Henry said apologetically.

The man said only "Oh" in the same tone of calm derision.

Fearful, not wanting to attract any more attention to himself, Henry fell silent.

Sifting through the forest, the troops spoke in low, sullen tones. The officers were impatient and snappy; their faces showed unhappiness. Once, a man in Henry's company laughed. A dozen soldiers quickly turned toward him and frowned with disapproval.

Ned fidgeted, cleared his throat, blushed, and said, "Henry, you might as well give me back those letters."

"All right." Henry loosened two buttons of his coat, thrust in his hand, and brought forth the packet.

Ned turned his face away as Henry reluctantly gave him the packet.

Ned's apparent shame increased Henry's self-esteem. *He* never had blushed with shame. He now viewed Ned with pitying condescension. Henry pictured himself returning home and telling a gaping audience of the blazing battles in which he had fought. His mother would cry out with horror and admiration. The young lady who had looked at him as he marched off to war would be awestruck.

CHAPTER 10

Henry heard musketry sputtering and cannons thudding. The 124th was marched to relieve a command that had been lying in damp trenches for a long time. The men took positions within a curving line of trenches. Before them was level ground dotted with deformed stumps. The dull popping of skirmishers and pickets firing in the fog came from the woods beyond. The noise of a terrific fracas came from the right.

The men sat behind the small embankments, awaiting their turn. Many had their backs to the firing. Ned lay down, buried his face in his arms, and quickly fell asleep. Henry leaned his chest against the brown dirt and peered over at the woods and up and down the line. Curtains of trees interfered with his view. He could see the low line of trenches for only a short distance. A few flags perched on the dirt hills. Behind them were rows of dark bodies with a few heads sticking curiously over the top.

The noise of skirmishers continued to c from the woods on the front and left. The di the right had grown to frightful proportions. guns were roaring without pause, too loud anyone's words to be heard.

At last the guns stopped. Dark rumor among the men in the trenches. The rumo of disasters, of hesitation and uncertainty part of those in charge. Bewildered by the news and not fully comprehending defe men were disheartened and began to mu

Before the sun's rays had completely ated the gray mists, the 124th was re through the woods. Enraged, Henry d "Our generals are blockheads!"

A man replied, "More than one fe said that today."

"I guess we got licked," Ned said Henry denounced General Hooke

"Maybe it wasn't his fault," Ned s ly. "He did the best he could." Ne along with stooped shoulders.

"Don't we fight like the devil? Do everything that men can?" Henry loudly. Secretly he was startled that those words. For a moment his face guilty look. But no one questioned say such words, and he quickly recov of courage. He went on to repeat

The noise of firing dogged the troops' footsteps. The men muttered and cursed, throwing black looks in its direction.

The troops finally were halted in a clear space. Regiments that had been separated and fragmented by encounters with thickets came back together. The lines were faced toward the noise of the Confederates' pursuing infantry. This noise increased to a loud burst and then, as the sun went serenely up the sky and threw illuminating rays into the gloomy thickets, became prolonged peals. The woods began to crackle. The men lay down behind whatever protection they could collect.

"I thought they'd attack as soon as the sun was well up," Lieutenant Hasbrouck said. Striding to and fro in the rear of his men, he repeatedly jerked at his little mustache.

Artillery, wheeled into position in the rear, shelled the distance. Unmolested, the 124th awaited the moment when lines of flame would slash the gray shadows of the woods in front of them.

"We're always being chased around like rats," Henry grumbled. "It makes me sick. Nobody seems to know where we go or why. We get licked here and licked there, and nobody knows why it's done. I'd like to know why the hell we were marched into these woods unless it was to give the rebels a good shot at us. We came in here and . . . "

Ned calmly interrupted. "It'll turn out all right."

"The devil it will!"

Hasbrouck fumed, "You boys, shut up! All you have to do is fight, and you'll get plenty of that in about ten minutes. Less talking and more fighting is what's best for you boys." He paused, ready to pounce on any man bold enough to reply. No one said anything, so he resumed his pacing.

The day had brightened. The sun's full radiance now shone on the crowded forest. A gust of battle came sweeping toward the 124th. The front shifted a bit to meet it squarely. There was a wait. In this part of the field the tense moments that precede a tempest slowly passed.

Having slept little and labored much, the regiment's men were exhausted. Some shrank and flinched as they stood awaiting the shock.

Henry felt rage and exasperation. He beat his foot on the ground and scowled at the swirling smoke that was approaching. He was sore and stiff. The Confederates' determination to give him no rest was maddening. He hated the relentless foe. He was not going to be harassed like a kitten chased by boys. If he was driven into a corner, he'd show his teeth and claws. "If they keep chasing us, they'd better watch out," he said to Ned.

Ned said calmly, "If they keep chasing us, they'll drive us into the river."

Henry crouched behind a small tree, his eyes burning hatefully and his teeth set in a cur-like snarl. His head still was bandaged. A spot of dry blood was over his wound. His hair was tousled; some locks hung down over the bandage. His jacket and shirt were open at the throat, exposing his young bronze neck. He gulped spasmodically. His fingers twined nervously around his rifle. He felt that he and his companions were being taunted and derided because they were poor and puny. He wanted revenge.

A single rifle flashed in a thicket before the 124th. In an instant many others joined it. A moment later the regiment roared forth its retort. Clashes and crashes swept through the woods. The guns in the rear returned shellfire. The battle roar settled to a rolling thunder. A dense wall of smoke slowly settled down, slit by knifelike rifle fire.

Henry was determined to defend his position behind the little tree against the entire world. The Confederates came on and on. Flames bit him; hot smoke broiled his skin. His rifle barrel grew so hot that ordinarily he couldn't have continued to hold it in his palms, but he kept on stuffing cartridges into it and pounding them with his clanking, bending ramrod. When he aimed through the smoke at some changing form, he pulled his trigger with a fierce grunt, as if he were dealing a fist blow with all his strength.

When the Confederates fell back, Henry sprang forward like a dog who becomes more aggressive when his foes begin to depart. When he was compelled to retire again, he did it slowly, sullenly, with wrathful despair. Once, so engrossed that he wasn't aware of a lull, he continued firing when all those near him had ceased.

Someone laughed hoarsely and called to him, "You damn fool. Don't you know enough to stop firing when there's nothing to shoot at?"

Henry then turned and saw his comrades staring at him. Turning back to the front he saw, under the lifted smoke, a deserted ground. For a moment he was bewildered. Then, comprehending, he said, "Oh." He returned to his comrades and threw himself onto the ground. He groped for his canteen.

Puffing out his chest with pride, Hasbrouck called out to Henry, "By God, if I had ten thousand wild cats like you, I could tear the stomach out of this war in less than a week!"

Some of the men muttered and looked at Henry with awe. They now regarded him as a war devil.

Ned came staggering to him. "Are you all right, Henry? Is there something wrong with you?"

"No," Henry said with difficulty. His throat seemed full of burs. He considered what he had done. He had fought like a beast. He regarded himself as a hero. He lay and basked in his comrades' occasional stares. To varying degrees their faces were black from burned powder. They reeked with perspiration and wheezed.

Hasbrouck walked up and down, restless and eager. "Hot work! Hot work!" he cried deliriously. Sometimes he laughed wildly.

"I bet this army never will see another new regiment like us!" one man said.

"You bet! They've lost a pile of men. If an old woman swept up the woods, she'd get a dustpanful."

"And if she'll come around again in about an hour, she'll get a pile more."

The rolling clatter of musketry came from off under the trees. Each distant thicket seemed like a porcupine with quills of flame. A cloud of dark smoke, as from smoldering ruins, went up toward the sun, which was bright in the blue sky.

CHAPTER
11

The ragged 124th had some minutes of respite, but during this pause the struggle in the forest became magnified. Trees seemed to quiver from the firing, and the ground seemed to shake from the rushing of men. The cannons' voices mingled in unceasing conflict. The men's chests strained for a bit of freshness; their throats craved water.

During this lull the men heard the screams of a man shot through the body. Maybe he had screamed during the fighting, but no one had heard him. Now the men turned to him.

"Who is it?"

"Jimmie Rogers."

Rogers thrashed in the grass, twisting his shuddering body into many strange postures. Screaming, he shrieked curses at the men.

Ned thought there might be a stream near-by. He got permission to go for some water. Immediately canteens were showered on him. "Fill mine, will you?" "Bring me some, too." "Me, too." Ned departed, loaded with canteens.

Hoping to throw his hot body into the

stream, soak there, and drink quarts, Henry went with Ned. They hurriedly searched but found no stream.

Henry and Ned began to retrace their steps. As they again faced the place of the fighting, they saw dark stretches winding along the land. In one cleared space a row of guns made gray clouds filled with flashes of orange flame. Over some foliage they saw a burning house. One window glowed a deep red. A tower of smoke from the house went far into the sky.

Looking over their own troops, Henry and Ned saw masses slowly getting into regular formation. The sunlight made twinkling points of the bright steel. To the rear was a distant roadway that curved over a slope. It was crowded with retreating infantry.

The smoke and noise of battle filled the forest. Shells hooted nearby. Occasional bullets buzzed in the air and bore into tree trunks. Wounded men and other stragglers slinked through the woods. Looking down an aisle of the grove, Henry and Ned saw General Vanderhof and his staff almost ride over a wounded man, who was crawling. Vanderhof reined strongly at his charger's open, foaming mouth and dexterously guided the horse past the man, who scrambled in wild haste. His strength apparently failed him as he reached a safe place. One of his arms weakened, and he fell, sliding over onto his back. He lay stretched out, breathing gently.

A moment later the small, creaking cavalcade was directly in front of Henry and Ned. Another general, riding with a cowboy's skillful abandon, galloped his horse to a position directly in front of Vanderhof and saluted. Unnoticed, Henry and Ned lingered nearby to overhear the conversation.

Vanderhof, who commanded Henry and Ned's division, looked at the other general and coolly said, "The enemy's forming over there for another charge, Meyers. It'll be directed against Whiterside. I fear they'll break through unless we work like thunder to stop them."

Meyers cleared his throat. "It'll be hell to pay to stop them."

"I presume so," Vanderhof remarked. "What troops can you spare?"

"I had to order in the 12th to help the 76th. But there's the 124th. They fight like a bunch of mule drivers. I can spare them the best of any."

Henry and Ned exchanged glances of astonishment.

Vanderhof spoke sharply. "Get them ready, then. I'll watch developments from here and send you word when to start them. It'll be in about five minutes."

Meyers saluted and wheeled his horse around. As he started away, Vanderhof called out to him in a sober voice, "I don't think many of your mule drivers will survive."

Meyers smiled and shouted something in reply.

Scared, Henry and Ned hurried back to the line. Henry now saw with new eyes. He was startled to learn that he was insignificant. Meyers spoke of the regiment with indifference, as he might refer to a broom. Part of the woods needed sweeping, and the men were the broom that would do that sweeping.

As Henry and Ned approached the line, Hasbrouck saw them and swelled with wrath. "Fleming! Wilson! How long does it take you to get water? Where have you been?" But his scolding ceased when he saw their wide eyes.

"We're going to charge!" Ned cried.

"Charge?" Hasbrouck said. "By God, that's real fighting!" A boastful smile lit his soiled face. "Charge? By God, we'll charge, then."

A small group of soldiers surrounded Henry and Ned. "Are you sure?" "Well, I'll be damned." "Charge? What for? At what?"

"We heard them talking," Ned said.

The men caught sight of two mounted fig-ures a short distance away. One was Colonel

MacChesnay. The other was Meyers. They were gesticulating at each other.

Pointing at them, Ned interpreted the scene.

The men accepted the situation. They thought about it and expressed many different sentiments. Many pulled their trousers a bit higher and tightened their belts.

A moment later the officers began to bustle among the men, pushing them into a more compact mass and better alignment. They chased those who straggled and fumed at a few who seemed rooted to their spots. They were like cowboys rounding up cattle.

The 124th seemed to draw itself up and heave a deep breath. The soldiers bent and stooped like sprinters before a signal. Their eyes peered from their grimy faces toward the curtains of the deeper woods. They were surrounded by the noises of the monstrous battle between the two armies.

Henry shot a quick, questioning glance at Ned, who returned the look. They were the only foot soldiers who knew the full truth: "mule drivers," "hell to pay," "I don't think many will survive." Still, they saw no hesitation in each other's faces. When a shaggy man near them meekly said, "We'll get swallowed," they just nodded.

Henry stared at the land in front of him. From the corners of his eyes he saw a young officer come galloping, waving his hat. The charge began. The men gave one great yell and lunged forward. The line fell slowly forward like a toppling wall. Henry was pushed and jostled for a moment. Then he lunged ahead and began to run.

Henry kept his eyes on a distant but prominent clump of trees. Thinking that the enemy must be there, he ran toward this clump as toward a goal. He ran desperately, wanting to get the matter over with as quickly as possible. His face was hard and tight with stress. He glared. He looked insane, with his soiled, disordered uniform; red, inflamed features; dirty head bandage; wildly swinging rifle; and banging equipment.

As the 124th swung out into a clearing, the woods and thickets ahead of it awakened. Yellow flames leaped toward the regiment from many directions. Bushes, trees, and uneven places on the ground scattered the regiment into clusters.

Henry still headed toward the clump of trees. The Confederates' clannish yell sounded from all the places near it. Rifle flames leaped from it. Bullets and shells shot through the air. One shell exploded in the middle of a hurrying group. One member of the group futilely threw up his hands to shield his eyes. Pierced by bullets, other men fell in grotesque agonies. The regiment left a trail of bodies.

Henry saw everything with extraordinary clarity. He seemed to see each blade of grass and the rough surface of every tree trunk. He seemed aware of every change in the thin, transparent vapor that floated in sheets. He saw men run madly and fall dead. He saw his comrades' starting eyes and sweating faces and heard their barbaric war cries. There was a kind of delirious defiance.

Presently the pace slackened. As if winded, the 124th began to falter and hesitate. Staring intently, the men began to wait for some of the distant walls of smoke to move and reveal the scene. No longer in their first burst of energy, they returned to caution. Henry believed that he had run miles.

The 124th ceased its advance. Halted, the men saw some of their comrades drop with moans and shrieks. A few lay underfoot, still or wailing. For an instant the men stood, their rifles slack in their hands, and watched the regiment dwindle. They appeared dazed. The spectacle seemed to paralyze them. They stared stupidly and looked from face to face. It was a strange pause and a strange silence.

Then Hasbrouck roared. He strode forth, his infantile features black with rage. "Come on, you fools!" he bellowed. "Come on! You can't stay here. Come on!" He yelled more, but his words couldn't be heard over the battle noise. While looking back over his shoulder at the men, he started forward. "Come on!" he yelled. The men stared at him with blank eyes. He was obliged to halt and retrace his steps. Standing with his back to the Confederates, he cursed at the men.

Ned roused. Lurching forward and dropping to his knees, he fired an angry shot at the persistent woods. This action awakened the men, who resumed firing. Belabored by their officers, they moved forward but in jolts, like a cart moving through mud. Every few paces the men stopped to fire and load. In this way they moved slowly from tree to tree.

The flaming opposition in front of them grew with their advance until it seemed that leaping tongues barred every way forward. Smoke hung in confusing clouds that made it difficult for the regiment to see. As he passed through each curling mass, Henry wondered what would confront him on the other side.

The 124th went painfully forward until an open space stood between them and the Confederate lines. Here the men crouched and cowered behind trees. They looked wild-eyed, like driven animals who don't understand where they're going or why. While they halted,

Hasbrouck again bellowed profanely. Despite the threatening bullets, he coaxed, berated, and cursed. Usually shaped in a soft, childlike curve, his lips writhed in unholy contortions. "Come on, you lunkheads!" he roared. "We'll all be killed if we stay here. All we have to do is cross that lot."

Hasbrouck strode down the regiment. Then, standing in front of the flag and waving his bandaged hand, he screamed, "Forward! Forward!"

As if obeying, the flag bent forward. For a moment the men wavered. Then, with a long wail, the dilapidated 124th surged forward over the field. Henry ran like a madman to reach the woods before a bullet could find him. He ducked his head like a football player. As he hurtled forward, he felt intense love for the flag that was near him. It seemed radiantly beautiful and indestructible because it couldn't be killed. As if to partake of its invulnerability, Henry stayed near it.

Suddenly the flag bearer flinched and faltered as if he'd been bludgeoned. Henry sprang and clutched at the pole. At the same instant Ned grabbed it from the other side. The flag bearer fell dead.

Henry and Ned briefly scuffled over the flag. "Give it to me!" "No, let me have it!" Each felt satisfied with the other's possession of the flag but also felt bound to declare his willingness to carry it, thereby placing himself at special risk. Henry roughly pushed Ned away.

Henry and Ned now saw that much of the regiment had crumbled away. Dejected, their force expended, the men were slowly retreating. They still faced the spluttering woods and replied to the din with their hot rifles.

"Where in hell are you going?" Hasbrouck howled.

A red-bearded officer commanded, "Shoot into them! Shoot into them! God damn their souls!"

The 124th fell back to trees. For a moment it halted there and blazed at some dark forms that had begun to steal up on it. Then it resumed its march, curving among the tree trunks. By the time the depleted regiment reached open space, it was receiving fast, merciless fire. It seemed encircled by mobs.

Discouraged and worn down, most of the men accepted the pelting of the bullets with bowed and weary heads. They felt betrayed, that they had been made to battle something unconquerable. They glowered at some of the officers. However, men in the regiment's rear continued to shoot irritably at the advancing Confederates.

Hasbrouck was perhaps the last man in the disordered mass. His back was toward the

Confederates. He had been shot in one arm, which hung straight and rigid. Occasionally he forgot his injury and started to emphasize some oath with a sweeping gesture. The multiplied pain caused him to swear with even greater force.

Henry went along on slipping feet. He kept watchful eyes rearward. He scowled with rage and mortification. He gazed with hatred at Meyers, who had called the men "mule drivers." Henry had wanted Meyers to regret his words and see that he was wrong. But Henry's dreams had collapsed when the regiment, rapidly dwindling, had hesitated in the small clearing and then recoiled. The retreat was a march of shame to him.

Keeping the flag erect, Henry harangued his fellows, pushing against their chests with his free hand. He frantically appealed to those he knew well, beseeching them by name. He felt a fellowship and equality with Hasbrouck, who also scolded and was mad with rage. The two supported each other in all sorts of hoarse, howling protests.

But the 124th was a rundown machine. The few soldiers who were reluctant to retreat saw their comrades hurry back to the lines. It was difficult to worry about one's reputation when others were worrying about surviving. Wounded men were left crying.

CHAPTER 12

No more firing threatened. There were colossal noises in the distance, but this part of the field was silent. The depleted band drew a long breath of relief and gathered to complete its trip. With anxious backward glances, the men hurried along, eager to avoid more danger.

As they approached their own lines, they were greeted with sarcasm by veterans who lay resting in the shade of trees. "Where the hell have you been?" "What did you come back for?" "Why didn't you stay there?" "Was it warm out there, sonny?" One veteran mockingly called to others, "Come quick and look at the soldiers!"

The bruised and battered 124th made no reply, except that one man broadcast challenges to fist fights, and the red-bearded officer glared at a tall captain in the other regiment. The remarks deeply stung Henry. He glowered with hatred at the mockers. But many in the 124th hung their

Peering through a rift in a smoke cloud, Henry saw a brown mass of apparently thousands of troops. A fierce-hued flag flashed before him. As if the smoke's clearing had been prearranged, the discovered troops immediately burst into a rasping yell, and a hundred flames jetted toward the retreating band. A rolling gray cloud again interposed as the regiment doggedly replied. Henry's ears buzzed from all the noise.

In the haze men panicked at the thought that the regiment was moving in the wrong direction. Those who headed the retreat turned and came pushing back against their comrades, screaming that they were being fired on from points that they had considered to be toward their own lines. Hysterical fear beset the troops. A soldier who previously had proceeded calmly now sank down and buried his face in his arms. Another shrilly lamented and cursed a general. Men ran here and there, seeking routes of escape.

Henry walked stolidly into the mob's midst. Holding the flag in both hands, he stood as if he expected an attempt to push him to the ground. He unconsciously assumed the attitude of the flag bearer in the previous day's fight.

Ned came up to him. "Well, Henry, I guess this is goodbye."

"Shut up, you damned fool!" Henry replied.

The officers labored to beat the mass of men

into a circle to face the menaces. The ground was uneven and torn. The men curled into depressions and fit themselves snugly behind whatever would frustrate a bullet. They waited for the smoke clouds to lift and reveal their enemy's location.

Henry noted with surprise that Hasbrouck was standing silently with his legs far apart and his sword held in the manner of a cane. Henry wondered why he didn't curse anymore. Suddenly the smoke lifted and Hasbrouck bawled, "Here they come! Right onto us, by God! Fire, men! Fire!" His further words were lost in a roar of thunder from the men's rifles.

Henry's eyes had instantly turned in the direction indicated by Hasbrouck. The Confederate troops were so near that Henry could see their features. He saw, with amazement, that their uniforms looked new. These troops apparently had been advancing cautiously, their rifles held ready, when Hasbrouck had discovered them and the volley from the blue regiment had interrupted their movement. Apparently they had been unaware of their foe's nearness. Almost instantly the smoke from Union rifles concealed the Confederates. Henry strained to see what the volley had accomplished, but the smoke hung before him.

Fast firings went back and forth. The men in blue were intent on revenge. Their dered valiantly. Their curving front b flashes and resounded with the clang ramrods. The Confederates shot bac ducked and dodged.

The Confederates' blows began to Fewer bullets ripped the air. Finally, w Union soldiers slackened, they saw onl floating smoke. The regiment gazed smoke coiled away, and the men saw a g empty of fighters. Twisted into fantastic sl a few corpses lay on the grass.

At this sight, many of the men in sprang from behind their covers and celebra with an ungainly dance of joy. Their eyes burl with tears. A hoarse cheer of elation broke fro their dry lips. They gazed around with looks pride, feeling new trust in the weapons in the hands. They felt like men again.

heads as if ashamed and trudged with new heaviness, as if bearing the coffin of their honor on their backs.

When the men arrived at their old position, they looked back at the ground over which they had charged. Henry was astonished to see that the distance was trivial. The trees where so much had happened seemed incredibly near. The time, too, had been short. He wondered at the number of emotions and events that had been crowded into such little space. It seemed then that the mockers were right. He glanced at his fellows with disdain. They were disheveled. Their features were red, swollen, and sweaty. They gulped at their canteens. However, Henry recalled his own actions with much satisfaction.

As the 124th lay heaving from its hot exertions, Meyers came galloping along the line. He had lost his cap. His tousled hair streamed wildly. His face was dark with anger. He jerked savagely at his horse's bridle, stopping the hard-breathing horse with a furious pull near MacChesnay. He immediately exploded in reproaches. "Damn it! You've made a mess of this, MacChesnay! Good Lord, man, you stopped about a hundred feet short of success! If your men had gone a hundred feet more, you would have made a great charge. As it is . . . What a bunch of mud diggers you've got!"

Listening intently, the men turned their curious eyes on MacChesnay, who straightened and looked insulted. But then he simply shrugged and said calmly, "We went as far as we could, General."

"As far as you could? Did you, by God?" Meyers snorted. "Well, that wasn't very far, was it?" He glanced into MacChesnay's eyes with cold contempt. "You were supposed to make a diversion to help Whiterside. Your own ears can tell you how well you succeeded." He wheeled his horse and rode stiffly away.

MacChesnay, hearing the jarring noises of an engagement in the woods to the left, broke out in vague damnations.

Having listened in impotent rage, Hasbrouck said, "I don't care if a man is a general. If Meyers says the boys didn't put up a good fight out there, he's a damned fool."

"Lieutenant," MacChesnay said sternly, "this is my own affair. I'll trouble you to ... "

Hasbrouck made an obedient gesture. "All right, Colonel." He sat down.

The news that Meyers had reproached the regiment went along the line. At first the men didn't believe it. When they began to believe that their efforts had, indeed, been dismissed as slight, they felt rebellious.

Ned said to Henry, "I wonder what the hell

Meyers wants. He must think we went out there and played marbles."

Henry said, "He probably didn't even see any of it. He just got mad as blazes and concluded that we're a bunch of sheep because we didn't do what he wanted."

"I've a notion to stay behind next time and let them take their charge and go to the devil."

Henry said soothingly, "We both did well. I'd like to see someone say we didn't do as well as we could."

"Of course we did," Ned declared. "I heard one guy say that you and I fought the best in the regiment. What I can't stand is those old soldiers laughing at us. And Meyers—he's crazy."

"He's a lunkhead!" Henry exclaimed. "He should come along next time. We'll show him what . . . "

Henry ceased because several men had come hurrying up. "Fleming, guess what we just heard?" one cried eagerly.

"Guess what we just heard?" the other repeated.

"What?" Henry asked.

Others made an excited circle.

"MacChesnay was talking to Hasbrouck right near us, and he said, 'By the way, who was the lad who carried the flag?' What do you think of that, Fleming? 'Who was the lad who carried the flag?' That's what he said. And Hasbrouck said, 'That was Fleming, and he's a jim-dandy.' And MacChesnay said, 'He is indeed. A very good man to have. He kept the flag way to the front.' And Hasbrouck said, 'Yes. He and Wilson were at the head of the charge and howling like Indians the whole time.' There, Wilson, my boy, put that in a letter and send it home to your mother, huh? And MacChesnay said, 'Were they indeed? Those two babies? At the head of the regiment?' 'Yes,' Hasbrouck said. 'They stayed at the head of the charge.' 'Well,' MacChesnay said, 'they deserve to be major generals.'"

"That's a lie," someone protested. "He never said that."

Henry and Ned blushed with pleasure. They exchanged a glance of joy and congratulations. They quickly forgot their previous fear, anger, and disappointment. Their hearts swelled with grateful affection for Hasbrouck and MacChesnay.

CHAPTER
13

When Confederates began to pour from the woods, Henry felt serene self-confidence. He smiled briefly when he saw Union soldiers dodge and duck the screeching shells thrown over them in giant handfuls. He stood, tranquil and erect, watching the attack begin against a part of the line that made a blue curve along the side of an adjacent hill.

A short way off he saw two regiments fighting a little separate battle with two other regiments. They fought in a cleared space. The firings were fierce and rapid. These intent regiments apparently were oblivious to all larger purposes of war and were slugging at each other as if in a team sport.

In another direction Henry saw a magnificent brigade go toward woods with the evident intention of driving the Confederates out. They passed out of sight, and there soon was an unspeakable racket in the woods. The brigade then marched out again, in a proud, unhurried way, with its fine formation intact.

A long row of guns on a slope to the left fired down onto the woods, where the Confederates were forming for another attack. The guns' round, red discharges produced a crimson flare and high, thick smoke. Henry occasionally glimpsed the toiling artillerymen. Behind the row of guns stood a house, calm and white amid bursting shells. Tied to a long railing, a group of horses frantically tugged at their bridles. Men ran here and there.

The detached battle between the two pairs of regiments lasted for some time. They struck at each other savagely. Then the Confederate regiments faltered and drew back, leaving the Union soldiers shouting.

Then there was stillness except for the faint thunder of artillery. The blue lines shifted a bit and stared expectantly at the silent woods and fields in front of them. The hush was solemn and churchlike.

Then a spluttering began in the woods. The guns on the slope roared in response. The noise quickly swelled to an interminable roar.

On a road that wound around an incline, Henry saw opposing forces move backwards and forwards in surges. Sometimes one side would cheer, then the other. Once, Henry saw

Confederates leap toward the Union lines. Another time a blue wave dashed with thunderous force against a gray obstruction, which was cleared away. In their swift, deadly rushes to and fro the men always screamed and yelled like maniacs.

Men quarreled over hiding places, such as trees and pieces of fence. Every instant, men desperately lunged at such protective spots.

When its time came, the emaciated 124th bustled forth with undiminished fierceness. When bullets again assaulted them, the men gave barbaric cries of rage and pain. With intent hatred they bent their heads behind their gun hammers. Their ramrods clanged with fury as they eagerly pounded cartridges into rifle barrels. The regiment's front was a smoke wall penetrated by yellow and red flashes.

Wallowing in the fight, the men soon were filthy again. Moving to and fro, jabbering, with blackened faces and glowing eyes, they were like fiends jigging in smoke.

Hasbrouck produced new curses suited to the emergency. He swung strings of expletives lash-like over the men's backs.

Still the flag bearer, Henry didn't feel idle. He was deeply absorbed as a spectator. The great drama's crash and swing made him lean forward, his face working in small contortions.

Sometimes he prattled, words coming unconsciously from him in grotesque exclamations. The flag hung silently over him.

A formidable line of Confederates came within dangerous range. Henry could see them plainly: tall, gaunt men running with long strides toward a rail fence. At the sight of this danger the Union soldiers ceased their cursing monotone. There was an instant of strained silence before they threw up their rifles and fired at the Confederates.

But the Confederates quickly gained the fence's protection. They slid down behind the fence and began to briskly slice up the blue men.

The Union soldiers braced themselves for a great struggle. Often, clenched white teeth shone from their dusky faces. The Confederates behind the fence frequently yelled taunts, but the 124th maintained a stressed silence. It was breathlessly intent on holding off the enemy. It fought swiftly and with a despairing savageness.

Henry had resolved not to budge whatever happened. If he died, his torn body would be a sharp reproach to Meyers.

The men grunted and dropped in bundles. An orderly of Henry's company was shot through the cheeks. His jaw hung far down, showing a pulsing mass of blood and teeth in the wide cavern of his mouth. He attempted to

cry out but couldn't. He ran to the rear, looking around wildly for aid. Others fell at their
companions' feet. Some of the wounded
crawled away. Many lay still, their bodies twisted into impossible shapes.

Henry looked for Ned. There he was: pow-
der-smeared and frazzled. Hasbrouck was
unharmed in his position at the rear. He still
cursed, but he seemed to be using his last box of
oaths. The 124th's fire had begun to decrease.
Hasbrouck's robust voice rapidly was growing
weak.

Followed by other officers, Colonel
MacChesnay came running along behind the
line. "Charge them!" the officers cried. "Charge
them! Push them away from the fence!"

To Henry's surprise, the weary and stiff
men immediately made ready. Bayonet shafts
rattled against rifle barrels. At the yelled words
of command, the soldiers sprang forward,
cheering. The dusty, tattered men ran toward
the fence, dimly outlined in smoke, where
enemy rifles spluttered.

Henry kept the flag to the front. Shrieking
appeals, he waved his free arm in furious circles.
Wild with unselfish enthusiasm, the mob of blue
men hurled themselves into the rifle fire. As
Henry ran, he anticipated a great crash when the
opposing troops would collide. Around him he

felt the regiment's onward swing.

Some Confederates ran. Others retreated more stubbornly. Individuals frequently wheeled around to fire at the blue wave. At one part of the line was a grim, stubborn group who didn't move. They were settled firmly down behind the fence. A ruffled flag waved over them, and their rifles dinned.

The blue whirl of men got very near. They yelled in rage at the disdainful group of men in gray. The two sides exchanged insults.

Henry gazed on the Confederate flag. Taking it would be a source of great pride. He plunged at it like a mad horse.

At close range the blue men halted and fired a swift volley. This fire split the group in gray. The men in blue yelled again and rushed in. Henry saw several stricken men tottering. The flag bearer was among them. Fatally shot, he hugged his precious flag and tried to stumble to safety.

Cheering, blue men leaped over the fence. Ned went over in a tumbling heap and sprang at the flag. Wrenching it free, he swung its red brilliance with a cry of exultation. Gasping, the flag bearer fell over, stiffened convulsively, and turned his dead face to the ground. There was much blood on the grass.

The men gesticulated and bellowed in ecstasy. They flung their hats into the air.

Four Confederates had been taken prisoner. Blue men circled them where they sat, asking them a flurry of questions. One prisoner had a superficial foot wound. He cuddled his foot as if it were a baby but often looked up at his captors and cursed them. Another prisoner, a mere boy, accepted his situation with calmness and apparent good nature. He conversed with the men in blue, studying their faces with his bright, keen eyes. The talk was of battles and conditions. Everyone was keenly interested in this exchange of viewpoints. The third captive sat with a cold, morose expression. His reply to every question and comment was the same: "Go to hell." The fourth prisoner remained silent. Looking mournful and ashamed, he kept his face turned away.

After the men had celebrated sufficiently, they crossed back over the fence and settled down alongside it. There was some long grass. Henry nestled in it and rested while a rail of the fence supported the flag. Jubilant and glorified, proudly holding his treasure, Ned came to Henry. They sat side by side and congratulated each other.

CHAPTER
14

The sounds that had stretched across the forest began to grow intermittent and weak. The artillery continued in some distant encounter, but the musketry all but ceased. Henry and Ned looked up and saw troops on the march. Artillery wheeled along at a leisurely pace. Many departing muskets gleamed on the crest of a small hill.

Henry got up. "What now?" He shaded his eyes with his grimy hand and gazed over the field.

Ned got up and stared. "I bet we'll go back over the river."

They waited, watching. The 124th was ordered to retrace its way. Grunting, regretting the end of soft repose, the men got up. They jerked their stiff legs and stretched their arms over their heads. One man swore as he rubbed his eyes. They all groaned, "Oh, God." They had as many objections to this change as they would have had to a new battle. They tramped back over the field across which they had madly run.

The 124th marched until it joined its fellows. The brigade formed a column and headed down a dusty road. The men trudged along parallel to the Confederates' lines. Then they curved away from the field and went toward the river. Realizing the significance of this movement, Henry breathed with new satisfaction. He nudged Ned and said, "It's over."

"By God, it is," Ned agreed.

Henry now cast off his battlefield mindset. His brain cleared. He understood that he had been in a world of red blood and black passion and he had escaped. He rejoiced. Then he reflected on his actions: his failures and achievements. He was happy. His publicly observed deeds paraded in great splendor. He joyfully recalled his comrades' admiring comments. Then he recalled his flight from the first engagement. For a moment he blushed with shame. He also recalled Dave. Gored by bullets and faint from blood loss, Dave had fretted about an imagined wound in a friend and had used his last strength and clearness of mind to help Jim. Henry had deserted Dave, helpless and delirious, in a field. At the thought that his misdeed might become known, Henry broke into a cold sweat. He gave one cry of grief.

"What's the matter, Henry?" Ned asked.

Henry replied with an outburst of swearing.

As he marched along the road, the vision of his cruelty clung to him.

The men around him plodded in ragged array, discussing with quick tongues the accomplishments of the late battle.

"We got a damn good licking."

"In your eye! We aren't licked. We're gonna swing around and come in behind them."

"Shut up with your 'come in behind them.' I've seen all I want to!"

"Bill Smithers says he'd rather have been in a thousand battles than in that hell of a hospital. He says they were shot at in the night and shells dropped right on the hospital. He says he never heard such screaming."

"Hasbrouck? He's the best officer in this regiment. The best."

"Didn't I tell you we'd come in behind them? Didn't I tell you so?"

"Oh, shut your mouth!"

For a time his persistent recollection of Dave robbed Henry of all elation. He vividly saw his error. He feared that it would stand before him the rest of his life. He didn't share in his comrades' chatter or even look at them. Gradually he managed to put his sin at a distance. His eyes opened to new ways. Previously he had taken pride in displayed heroics. Now he despised bravado. He felt a quiet manhood, strong but unaggressive. Whatever came, he would meet it with inner strength. As he trudged from the place of blood and rage, his soul changed. He passed from wrath to tranquility.

It rained. The procession of weary soldiers became a bedraggled train, despondent and muttering, marching in mud under a low, wretched sky. But Henry smiled. For him the world was new. He had rid himself of battle's red sickness. The sultry nightmare was over. He had been an animal blistered and sweating in war's heat and pain. He turned now with a lover's thirst to images of tranquil skies, fresh meadows, and cool brooks: soft and eternal peace. Over the river a golden ray of sun came through the leaden rain clouds.

AFTERWORD

About the Author

In *The Red Badge of Courage* author Stephen Crane says of Henry Fleming, "He had dreamed of battles all his life—vague conflicts of thrilling sweep and fire. He had imagined himself bravely protecting people and gaining glory. Several times he had burned to enlist. He had read of marches and battles and had longed to see it all." Crane could have been describing himself.

Like Henry, Crane "dreamed of battles" from an early age. He was born in Newark, New Jersey in 1871, the youngest of fourteen children. His father, Jonathan Townley Crane, was a Methodist minister who wrote books on religion and ethics. His mother, Mary Helen Peck Crane, wrote articles on a wide range of subjects, including religion and family life. Nevertheless, military things fascinated Crane from childhood. As a boy he often played soldier. While living in Port Jervis, New York from

1878 to 1880, he frequently listened to veterans recount their Civil War experiences. Similarly, Henry eagerly absorbs the tales of battle-tried soldiers who relate their encounters with "smoke, fire, and blood."

Before Henry leaves home, his mother urges him not to drink or swear, reminding him that his father never drank liquor and rarely cursed. Crane's parents, too, disapproved of drinking and swearing. Both of them wrote and publicly spoke on the evils of alcohol. Just as Henry disregards his mother's plea and readily curses, Crane routinely swore and drank.

"Many women have to bear up after the loss of their husbands and sons," Henry's widowed mother comments. It's easy to imagine Crane's mother expressing the same sentiment. She was widowed when Crane was eight; she also outlived a number of her sons. Henry's mother finds strength in her religious beliefs. When Henry last glimpses her, she is kneeling in prayer. Crane's mother, too, was deeply religious.

From 1888 to 1890, Crane attended a military school, Claverack College in upstate New York. Many of his teachers were Civil War veterans who shared their memories of the conflict. Before Henry goes off to war, his schoolmates crowd around him and admire him in uniform; he "swells" with pride and "struts." Similarly,

Crane excited much attention when he returned home to Asbury Park, New Jersey one summer wearing his Claverack uniform. At Claverack, Crane participated in numerous military drills. Perhaps he was recalling his own frustration when he later wrote, "Henry had come to see himself as simply part of a vast uniformed demonstration. He was drilled and drilled."

Henry volunteers for combat. In 1897 Crane tried to enlist to fight in the Spanish-American War. (The army rejected him because he was physically unfit.)

But Crane's chief passion was writing. He wrote his first poem at age six and first short story at eight. As a teenager he contributed articles to newspapers, including the prestigious *New York Tribune*. When he attended Syracuse University for one semester in 1891, he failed five of his six courses but got an A in English literature. In 1891 he moved to Manhattan to work as a freelance writer. He self-published his first novel, *Maggie: A Girl of the Streets*, in 1893.

Inspired by Civil War accounts that Crane had heard and read, *The Red Badge of Courage* followed in 1895, when Crane was twenty-three. A bestseller, the book brought Crane international fame. Although he had no personal experience of war, the novel was acclaimed for its realism.

Crane next wrote travel articles on the American West and Mexico. Having sought assignments in combat areas, he then reported from the front lines on the Greco-Turkish War in Greece and the Spanish-American War in Cuba.

In 1897 Crane moved to England with writer Cora Taylor, whom he had met in Florida the year before. Three of his most highly regarded short stories appeared in 1898: "The Bride Comes to Yellow Sky," "The Blue Hotel," and "The Open Boat."

Crane died of tuberculosis in 1900, at age twenty-eight. In his short life he created numerous poems, articles, essays, short stories, and novels that continue to be widely read and greatly admired.

Henry starts out dreaming of glory on the battlefield. It was Crane the writer, not Henry the fighter, who achieved renown.

About the Book

The Red Badge of Courage depicts nature as peaceful and holy when undisturbed by human violence. A scene of sunlight, vegetation, insects, and birds illustrates "the religion of peace." A "cathedral" light illuminates a forest. High, arching boughs form a "chapel" that glows in a "religious" half-light. Rustling trees sing a "soft hymn." Silent insects seem to be praying. When warfare temporarily ceases, a "solemn and churchlike" hush replaces the hellish clamor. War is the opposite of sacred tranquility: profane, diabolical, chaotic, insane, dehumanizing, savage, and grotesque.

Throughout the book, soldiers use profane language. They tell others to "be damned," "go to hell," and "go to the devil." A lieutenant bellows "profanely," his lips moving in "unholy" contortions. Another officer yells, "Shoot into them! God damn their souls!" Suggesting pagan idolatry, Stephen Crane refers to war as a "red animal" and "blood-swollen god." His message seems clear: maiming and killing are sacrilege.

Crane describes war as hellish. It brims with "deviltry." Soldiers frequently suffer from intense heat. In combat, Henry is bitten by flames, his skin "broiled" by hot smoke. Soldiers take on devilish characteristics. Their faces redden from heat, strain, and blood. In the midst of battle, with "blackened faces and glowing eyes," they resemble "fiends jigging in smoke." At night, silhouetted against the red light of their campfires, they look "weird and satanic."

As traditionally envisioned, hell is chaotic. Crane shows the chaos of war. Soldiers continually struggle to see through smoke that conceals even nearby people and objects. The tremendous noise of battle prevents men from hearing words and getting their bearings: "Men ran every which way. Artillery boomed before, behind, to the left, and to the right, destroying a sense of direction." In the confusion, men get separated from their regiments. Fighting and fleeing troops are "disordered," "mob-like," and "wild."

The chaos is psychological as well as physical. Men look "insane," run like madmen, and scream "like maniacs." They laugh hysterically, talk incoherently, and babble deliriously. Some literally go crazy. Often, soldiers fall into irrational rage. At one point Henry feels anger even toward his rifle. Henry's brain clears only when the fighting has stopped.

Fighting dehumanizes the combatants. Henry fights "like a beast," a "wild cat." Crane frequently compares the soldiers to nonhuman animals. To erect protective mounds, veterans hurriedly dig like terriers. Terrified men stare with "sheep-like eyes" and run like rabbits. Henry feels like "a driven beast." Cattle, mules, and other "driven beasts" lack freedom of choice. They must go where humans force them to. Henry, too, is powerless. He must follow orders. Without knowing the reasons behind his regiment's movements, he must go where his officers command. In war, lower-ranking soldiers lack free will. For a time Henry fears that the members of his regiment will be "slaughtered like pigs." Pigs sent to slaughter are helpless; they have no means of escape.

Removed from the influences of civilian society that encourage gentleness and kindness, soldiers easily lose all compassion and self-restraint. Henry deserts Dave, helpless and delirious, in a field. Some officers consign men to death with callous indifference. One officer speaks of Henry's regiment "as he might refer to a broom. Part of the woods needed sweeping, and the men were the broom that would do that sweeping." He smiles when another officer remarks that most of the regiment's men probably won't survive. In combat, soldiers give "barbaric" cries and strike at each other "savagely." Henry's bloody wound— his "red badge of courage"—comes not from battle but from a fellow Union soldier who senselessly bashes him on the head with a rifle butt.

Far from glorious, wounding and death are agonizing and grotesque. Shot through his body, one soldier thrashes in the grass, "twisting his shuddering body into many strange postures" while shrieking curses at others in his regiment. An orderly shot through his cheeks tries to cry out but can't. His jaw hangs down, exposing a cavernous mouth that is "a pulsing mass of blood and teeth." In his death throes, Jim shakes and stares. His eyes roll. Leg tremors cause him to dance "a hideous hornpipe. His arms beat wildly about his head as if in enthusiasm." When he crashes to earth, his body bounces. In death his mouth bears the shape of a laugh. Henry comes upon a corpse that has gray skin, glazed eyes, an open mouth of "appalling yellow," and ants swarming over its face.

Having previously valued "displayed heroics," at the end of the novel Henry has matured into someone who cherishes peace. As he leaves the battleground, he passes "from wrath to tranquility." He has "rid himself of battle's red sickness," "war's heat and pain." The "nightmare" is over. Now he rejoices in "tranquil skies, fresh meadows, and cool brooks: soft and eternal peace."